Stupid Cupid

Stupid Cupid

Rhonda Stapleton

SIMON PULSE
New York London Toronto Sydney

SIMON PULSE
An imprint of Simon & Schuster Children's Publishing Division
1230 Avenue of the Americas, New York, NY 10020
First Simon Pulse paperback edition December 2009

For information about special discounts for bulk purchases, please contact Simon & Schuster Special Sales at 1-866-506-1949 or business@simonandschuster.com.
The Simon & Schuster Speakers Bureau can bring authors to your live event. For more information or to book an event contact the Simon & Schuster Speakers Bureau at 1-866-248-3049 or visit our website at www.simonspeakers.com.
Designed by Paul Weil
The text of this book was set in Caslon.
Manufactured in the United States of America
2 4 6 8 10 9 7 5 3 1
Library of Congress Control Number 2009934854
ISBN 978-1-4169-7464-2
ISBN 978-1-4169-9837-2 (eBook)

This is dedicated to my two crazy kids, Bryan and Shelby, who remind me every day how much fun it is to make people laugh. And to Bryan Jones, who more than once has turned a blind eye to my übermessy writing desk and has supported me every step of this journey.

Acknowledgments

Writing a novel, like raising children, takes the efforts of an entire village. Luckily, I have some pretty cool people in my corner.

A most heartfelt thanks to my agent, Caryn Wiseman, for believing in me. Your guidance in my writing career has been a lifeline, and I am grateful for your patience and help.

My editor, Anica Rissi, is truly magnificent—thank you for your keen editorial eye and brilliant ideas on my writing. You saw the spark in my novel and took a chance on me, and I'll never forget it.

Thanks to my parents, Pat and Ron; my sister, Lisa; Forrest and Lynne Jones; and all of my friends and family for encouraging me to follow my dreams, even if I changed my mind four billion times in the process.

A huge thanks to my kids and to Bryan, for keeping things running around the house while my brain is in writing la-la land.

Finally, for Deanna Carlyle, Amanda Brice, The Fictionistas, The Superhotties, The Blueboarders, Romance Divas, and Debut 2009 (A Feast of Awesome)—thank you for being such warm, welcoming writers. You've always been there whenever I've been in writerly full-blown panic mode and needed chocolate and hugs. You rock.

Chapter 1

"So"—Janet glanced down at my résumé—"Felicity. You'd like to be a matchmaker. Can you go into more detail why?"

Because my mom threatened bodily harm unless I get off my lazy butt and get a job. No, that wouldn't do. Better to try for the more professional approach.

"Well, I believe in true love," I replied. "I think everyone has a match out there—some people just need a little help finding that special person. I think it would be fun to do that."

Janet smiled, her bright, white teeth sparkling in the soft light pouring from the window. "Good answer. That's what we believe too. Here at Cupid's Hollow we want to find true love for everyone."

I nodded, trying not to fidget with the clicky end of my pen.

This was my first real interview, and I was determined not to let my twitchy thumb get the best of me. After applying for a thousand jobs (and getting a thousand rejections), I'd found a tiny ad on the back page of Cleveland's *Scene* magazine: TEEN CUPIDS WANTED FOR MATCHMAKING COMPANY. CALL FOR INTERVIEW.

It was a cute angle to advertise for employees in that way, so I called. Two days later, here I was. In all my nervous, sweaty glory, working it as best as I could so I wouldn't look or sound like a total idiot.

"So, you're a junior," Janet said. "And what school do you go to again?"

"Greenville High. Go, Cougars!" I cheered, then winced internally at my dorkiness. Oh, man, that was way lame. Like she cared about our school mascot. *I* didn't even care most of the time.

"Um-hm," she said, her face unreadable. She flipped through the notepad on her lap and scribbled furiously on a page.

Crap, did I blow it already? Three minutes into the interview and I'd sunk my own battleship.

"And you're available to start work . . . ?"

"As soon as possible," I spilled out, heart racing. Maybe this could still work out.

"Have you ever used a BlackBerry or similar handheld technology before?"

"Well, my mom has one, and I've used it a little bit." Okay, that was an exaggeration, as I've really only *seen* her use it, but I'm sure I could figure it out if I needed to.

Janet wrote more notes. "I assume you've never participated in or worked for a matchmaking service before?"

"Um, no." I thought fast. "But I did help my brother set up his Match dot com profile."

My brother is four years older than me and is a cop. Trust me, not a good combination. He's insane. I can't count the number of times he's flashed his stupid badge at me in front of my friends, threatening to haul me in if I mocked his authority again. Total dork.

"Okay, last question. This job requires a certain level of . . . confidentiality." Janet looked straight into my eyes, her face serious. "Confidentiality for our clients, as well as for our own technologies and processes. You'd have to sign a document promising never to share our information with anyone outside the company. Would that be a problem?"

I swallowed. What was I getting myself into here? Was this normal?

Geez, chill, Felicity. She wasn't asking me to sew my lips together and join a convent. They probably just didn't want other matchmaking companies to steal their ideas or customers.

I nodded and put on my most serious, trustworthy face. "Sure, no problem." A thought popped into my mind. "Wait, I'm only seventeen. Is the contract legally binding?"

She shot me a smile. "Good question. It's binding as far as our concerns go."

"Okay, then." Not that I'd be spilling any industry secrets, anyway, so I wouldn't have to worry about that.

Janet finished writing, then uncrossed her legs and smoothed her prim, plum-colored skirt. She stood and stuck out her hand. "Well, we'd love to have you join our team. Welcome to Cupid's Hollow, Felicity."

I bit back my squeal and shook her hand. "This is so awesome. Thank you!"

She grinned. "Why don't you come in tomorrow for the training session."

I thanked her profusely, slipped on my thick winter coat, and left the office, turning back to give the building one last glance. The outside itself was nondescript, just an old brick exterior with lots of windows and a thin layer of late March snow perched on top. But the inside held the key to my working future.

My first real job. I was so excited, I did a little booty shake in the parking lot. I couldn't wait to tell everyone I knew! If I'd had a cell phone, I could have called my best friends Maya and Andy instead of waiting until I got home. With a job, though, I would now be able to use my own money to buy one.

I hopped into my mom's dark green Camry, cranked up the heat and the radio, and headed home, taking the long way through the suburbs instead of driving on Route 480. Mom had let me borrow the car for the interview, but made me swear a solemn oath that I would not go anywhere but to the interview and back, would not pick up any hitchhikers, and would stay off the freeway at all costs.

"Mom," I said as soon as I threw open the front door, "I'm home. I got the job!" On the front porch I stomped the loose snow off my heels, then stepped into the foyer and gingerly slipped out of my boots. After tucking them into the corner of the tiled entryway and hanging my coat in the closet, I added, "And no, I didn't track snow in the house." I knew what she was going to ask, because it was the same thing every time.

Mom darted out of the kitchen, wearing a white apron over

her dress pants. Other than a small smudge of flour on her cheek, she looked pristine and composed, as usual. "Congratulations!" she cried out. "I'm so proud of you." She leaned over and kissed me on the cheek.

My mom is surprisingly domestic—she's as assertive in the kitchen as in her workplace, where she's in the accounting department. God help any of the company's clients who are late on their payments, because my mom hounds them until they pay, just to shut her up. She runs our household the same way.

When we were younger, my brother and I used to call her the House Nazi. Neither one of us was stupid enough to say it directly to her face, though—I liked my mouth right where it was, thank you very much.

"Thanks, Mom. What's for dinner?" I asked. "I'm starving to death."

"Fried chicken, but it's not ready yet. You should go call Maya and Andy with your good news. They'll be thrilled."

"Yup, I'm heading up to my room now." I tossed the keys on the small table in the foyer. "Thanks for letting me borrow the car."

She winked. "Well, now you can save up and get your own, can't you."

Gee, I'd suspected she'd say that. Now that I had a real job, I could predict the answer for everything:

Need new clothes, Felicity? Want to go see a movie with your friends? Well, it's a good thing you've got a job now.

I darted up to my room, flung myself across my bed, and grabbed the phone off my nightstand, dialing Andy's cell.

"Andy's mortuary. You stab 'em, we slab 'em."

Andy Carsen is my best friend. She and I have been close since kindergarten. Sometimes, though, I feel a bit jealous of her. Her folks aren't as harsh as mine can be. And Andy, of course, has a cell phone, just like everybody else I know. I swear, I must be the only teenager in the free world who doesn't have one. But now that I had a job, that was going to change.

"Hey, it's me."

"So . . . ?"

"I got the job!"

She squealed. "That's awesome! Now you'll finally have spending money, and we can go shopping more and buy those cute jeans you wanted and—"

"Whoa." I laughed. "I haven't even gotten a paycheck yet."

"So, how does this gig work? Will you make those geeky

videotapes of people, or is it an online dating thing?"

Hm. I hadn't even bothered to ask. "Actually, I don't know. I was so excited I got the job, I just took off before she could change her mind."

"You're ridiculous."

"You say that like you're surprised. Anyway, tomorrow I've got training, so I'll let you know."

We hung up, and I dialed Maya Takahashi, my other BFF. Maya moved to Cleveland when we were in middle school, and though she's completely unlike me or Andy in just about every possible way, we clicked. Maybe it was the way she quietly snarked on the preps her first day of school that made me instantly love her. From then on, the three of us have been nearly inseparable.

"'Lo," Maya said into the mouthpiece, her mouth clearly full of food.

"Hey," I answered. "I got the job!"

"That's great. I knew you would."

I heard her chew a few times, so I held the phone away from my ear to let her finish the bite without subjecting me to it. Delicate, she was not, but that was Maya for you.

"Sounds like you're busy," I said. "I'll let you go."

"Sorry, I'm totally stressing over here and trying to multitask by eating and doing homework at the same time. I almost bit off my pen cap! And then, after dinner, I need to practice my solo."

Maya's a fantastic trumpet player, in addition to all her brain talents. Though I'm not a huge fan of the school band—nerd alert, anyone?—Andy and I do support her and go see all her performances at the school's basketball games. I know she'd do the same for us.

"Okay, hope you get it all done. Talk to ya later."

After we hung up, I turned on my PC and logged on to my blog. I made sure to lock it so it was a VIP entry only—Andy, Maya, and I usually shared entries with only each other.

I'm so excited. Now that I'm a matchmaker, maybe I can even learn some tips to make Derek fall madly in love with me.

I sighed. Derek Peterson's the hottest guy on the face of the earth. Every time I look at him, my heart squeezes up, and I forget how to speak. Not that he ever talks to me, anyway. He's a smart jock who runs with the AP crowd (shame of all shame, I'm only in honors, not advanced), but we have art class together.

Of course, that's my favorite class, even though I end up spending the whole time trying not to get busted for staring at him. Or drooling.

I bet half my blog was filled with his name. I'd been crushing on him since the first day of freshman year, when I saw him walking through the hallway at school. Not that he'd noticed me, but it didn't matter. One look at his beautiful smile, and I was a goner.

Derek Peterson-n-Felicity Walker 4-ever

Mr. and Mrs. Derek Peterson

Felicity Walker-Peterson

Felicity Walker-Peterson, M.D.

Felicity Walker-Peterson, President of the United States

Felicity Walker-Peterson, America's Next Top Model

Well, that was fun. I saved and closed the blog, then quickly checked my e-mail (nope, nothing new, except from my spam buddies telling me I won the Irish lotto—lucky me!). Time to start my homework to avoid being grounded for getting anything below a C.

The next day at the office, Janet handed me a hot-pink PDA. "Here ya go," she said. "Your LoveLine 3000. Please take care of it. It's the key to your job."

Whoa. It was possibly the most tricked-out PDA I'd ever seen in my life. There had to be some serious dough coughed up for these puppies.

I sat in the plush green chair across from Janet's cherry wood desk, flipping on the device and looking at all the buttons. "So, what's this for? Are we supposed to schedule the customers' first dates or something?"

She tilted her head and gave me a funny look. "It has the e-mail addresses of everyone in your territory, which in your case is Greenville High."

"Wait. I'm matchmaking my school?" I didn't know yet if that was a good or a bad thing, so I tried to keep my voice calm and neutral.

"Absolutely. That's part of the reason we're hiring. We decided to try a new venture and let people matchmake their own peer groups. After all, who better to be a cupid for a teen than another teen?"

"Good point." Most of my classmates would die laughing if an adult tried to help them find a date. And with good reason.

I mean, no disrespect to anyone, but "great personality" can only get you so far in high school.

For instance, look at me. I've got personality practically oozing out of my skin, but I've only had one boyfriend ever. And he dated me so he could get closer to Andy. I should have picked up the clue phone when he always wanted to do group things—with her tagging along, of course. And here I'd thought he was just getting to know my friends.

Andy, of course, has no problems getting a guy's attention. She's hot, smart, and funny, but she's also extremely picky, so she doesn't date a lot. And she's 100 percent loyal to her friends, so my ex's strategy to get closer to her backfired, to say the least.

Poor Maya, on the other hand—the girl's sharp as a tack, captain of the debate club, lead trumpet in the marching band, but can't get a date to save her life. In fact, she can't even get a guy to notice her. Not that she'd even admit to wanting a boyfriend.

And not that she isn't cute enough, either. It's just . . . she's busy. And kinda shy. But still, I couldn't exactly picture her signing up with a dating service for help. That just isn't how it's done.

Janet delicately cleared her throat. "Felicity, this is no small thing. It's taken the company thousands of years to evolve and perfect our technology, but I like the way the PDAs work so far."

"I'm sorry, what did you say?" I must have misheard her. Maybe I needed to pay better attention to this training session instead of thinking about me and my friends' dating disasters.

"Trust me," she continued, chuckling, "you'll like using this much better than the bows and arrows of yesteryear. The misfiring possibility alone made the job more difficult than it needed to be. And the PDAs are far less cumbersome to carry."

I swallowed hard. Okay, I hadn't misunderstood. The lady was obviously a loony-bird.

And I was now employed by her.

I glanced at the door, trying to think of a polite way to get the hell out of there.

Janet paused, looking at me. "Are we on the same page here?"

I slid my eyes back to her face. "I—I'm guessing not." Because I was on planet Earth, and Janet was obviously circling somewhere around Jupiter, floating on a pink cloud with rainbows, bunnies, and fluffy kitty cats. And a whole lotta bathtub-created meth.

No wonder they always warned us to stay away from drugs.

Janet spoke slowly. "You do understand you're a cupid now, right?"

Chapter 2

"I'm . . . Cupid?" I squirmed in my seat.

She laughed hard for several seconds. "What? No."

I sagged in relief—I *had* misunderstood her.

"You're not Cupid. You're *a* cupid. There's more than one of us, you know."

"Well, okay, then." I stood before she could do something else crazy, like carve my name on her hand with a ballpoint pen. "It's been really nice meeting you, but I should go now."

Janet squinted at me, then stood, as well. "You're a skeptic. That's okay—almost all new hires are. Follow me."

She paced across her office and opened the door, hurrying into the hallway. Did she really expect me to follow her? This was my perfect chance to escape. I flung my coat on, struggling to slip my arms through the armholes as fast as I could. After snatching my purse from underneath the seat, I stepped outside of her office, then paused.

What if she was telling the truth? What if she really could prove to me I was a cupid? Or, more likely, what if she was loony but harmless, and I was missing out on the second half of a really great story to tell Andy and Maya? Before I realized what I was doing, I found myself heading down the hallway too, following the *click-clack* of her heels and trying to keep up.

I hoped I wasn't walking blindly into my own death. Mom would be so pissed if I did something dumb like that.

We hoofed it to the end of the hall and swung a left, going into a windowless room. Janet closed the door behind me.

"Take a look around," she said.

The glint of gold caught my eye immediately. There had to be millions of dollars' worth of antique weaponry here—namely, bows and arrows.

Janet picked out one bow and arrow and, quicker than the blink of an eye, pointed the arrow at me, firing it right into my chest.

"Aaaaaaaah!" Squeezing my eyes shut, I touched my tingling chest and looked down. No arrow sticking out of my heart. Not even a hole. The arrow had disappeared. "What the—?" I choked back the fearful sob building in my throat. "That's not funny. How'd you . . . ?"

She offered me a chagrined smile. "Sorry, but that's quite possibly the most effective way to show you. Magical arrows. They disappear when they hit their target. I told you, it's real." She hung the bow back on the wall. "Oh, and don't worry. You won't be falling in love. A matching arrow also has to be fired at someone else for the love spell to work. It's kind of like completing the electrical love circuit. That weird tingle you're feeling should wear off in an hour or so."

All I could do was gape as Janet led me out of the room and shut off the light, then locked the door behind us. We headed back to her office, me much more somber than before.

How was this even possible? How could she fire an arrow at me and have it disappear? I'd seen her shoot me with my own two eyes. But nothing had hit. I touched my chest again, the tingle reminding me I hadn't imagined things.

It seemed like there was no way to rationalize the incident other than to realize maybe it was true. I was Cupid. No, wait, *a* cupid.

About a billion questions flew into my head. How long had Janet been a cupid? How was she chosen? Was the knowledge just handed down from one cupid to the next? How did this all get started in the first place?

Then, it hit me: This had to be the coolest thing ever to happen to me. Even better than when I won tickets from a radio station to see Panic At The Disco in concert—from the front row, thank you very much.

Yeah, this crushed that little triumph right into the dust.

"Do I get wings?" I asked. If so, I hoped I got to pick out a pair of pretty ones. Maybe a nice sage green or pale purple. Or maybe she'd touch my back and they'd sprout out of my spine.

I shivered at the odd thought.

Janet snorted. "I wish. Unfortunately, that's a myth. Cupids can't fly. They're just imbued with magical properties for matchmaking."

Magic. It couldn't exist . . . could it? My tingly chest taunted me with the answer.

A sudden thrill of excitement shot through me. Oh my God, I couldn't wait to tell every—

"Nope," Janet said, sitting back in her executive chair. She chuckled. "I can read your face like a book. Looks like it's time to go over the rules."

"Okay." So being a cupid came with rules, just like everything else. I guess it made sense—you wouldn't want employees going crazy all over the place and hooking up people and chickens, or anything else weird like that.

"Rule number one. No one can know you're a cupid. Not your mom, not your best friend, not anyone. Sorry, but it compromises our anonymity. It's in the contract you signed, so don't even think about admitting it to anyone outside the company, ever, or else . . . well, let's just say don't."

I nodded in agreement. "Okay. I'll definitely keep my mouth shut." It would be hard, because I knew me. I'd want to spill the beans to Andy and Maya. But I wasn't about to double-cross a woman with magic arrows.

Weird. My friends and I never had any big secrets from each other. I hoped this wouldn't cause any issues. I'd have to come up with something to tell them about my job that wouldn't cause more questions.

Janet glanced at the PDA in my hand. "Oh, and don't lose your LoveLine 3000 or show anyone what's on it. If someone else tries to open it, it'll have only your school schedule, nothing else. We installed a custom security system, just to cloak the data." She smirked proudly.

Geez. This stuff was no joke. "I'll keep it close to me."

Janet nodded in approval. "Good. Now, rule number two. Only match your target to one other person at a time, making sure all matches meet the minimum-compatibility requirements of at least three common interests—but the more commonalities, the better. One pairing at a time, and if the love match doesn't last after the magic wears off in two weeks, you can try pairing the target with someone else."

"Okay." I took a mental note to write all of these rules down later.

"And last, rule number three. While you remain in our employment, you're not allowed to matchmake yourself. Sorry, it's a conflict of interest."

Well, crap. My dreams of Derek and me growing old together and holding hands on a rickety porch swing flushed down the drain right before my eyes. Because without a little magic, that was never going to happen. I sighed deeply. "All right."

"Great." Janet beamed, her mauve lipstick perfectly framing bright white teeth. "You are required to make at least one match per week, but the more matches you make, the better chance you'll have of creating lasting matches. Your minimum quota is one lasting match a month."

Only one a month? This was going to be a piece of cake. "Okay, so how will I know if it's a lasting match?"

"Lasting love matches keep going after the magic wears off in two weeks. We offer bonuses for those, so that's where the real money is. It's in your best interest, then, to pair up suitable people from the start."

"Okay, I see."

Janet opened a drawer in her desk and rummaged through it. "Be sure to read your instruction guide before attempting to create a compatibility chart or client profile. Your LoveLine 3000 has the capacity to store thousands of profiles, so start doing some investigatory work, and match well. But, most importantly, trust your gut. Aha, here we go." She pulled out a thick pamphlet and gave it to me.

"This is the guide on how to use the PDA to matchmake," she continued. "Basically, you'll send an e-mail to the target, and carbon-copy the compatible love interest. When they open the e-mail, it'll appear blank, but *Bam*!" She wiggled her fingers in the air. "Love at first byte. Get it?"

I forced a laugh. "Yeah, I get it." Sounded easy enough. I could totally do this.

Janet handed me her business card. "Call me if you get into trouble. And take it slow until you feel comfortable. *Read the instruction guide*—it'll help." She smiled. "Any other questions?"

I scrunched up my face, thinking. "Actually, yeah. If customers aren't paying for us to matchmake them, how does Cupid's Hollow make any money?"

She laughed. "We get sponsorship from companies that most benefit from love matches—the floral industry, the greeting card companies, and so on. They fund us, and we fund them. It works out nicely."

Sneaky. I never would have thought. "Makes sense, I guess."

Janet stood. "Okay. Well, if there aren't any other questions, go out there and make some matches!"

After third period the next day, I tossed my biology book and matchmaking instruction guide into my locker, grabbed my bagged lunch, and slammed the locker door, trying my best not to feel guilty for once again ditching the required cupid reading. I still hadn't gotten past the first few pages of the manual, which was littered with snoozeville statistics and compatibility rules . . . and about a billion teeny, tiny charts.

I consider myself a pretty smart person, but the material went right over my head. Did Janet really expect me to get all this stuff?

The highest quotient of compatibility cofactors increases optimal relationship longevity, give or take a 3 percent margin of error based on certain established external parameters, blah blah blah.

And that was just on page one.

After spending two hours last night reading the same few paragraphs over and over, I'd finally just decided to forge my own matchmaking path as best I could. I'd work on making minimum-compatibility matches for people I didn't know well and do in-depth matches for closer acquaintances.

This would increase my overall chances of a lasting match and save on research time, to boot. I mentally patted myself on the back for coming up with this brilliant strategy.

I whipped out my PDA and leaned back into the corner of an edge locker and a wall, scrolling through the profiles I'd been working on that morning. I'd never have expected how much pressure I would feel to make my matches good ones. This was serious stuff. I'd spent all morning in between classes scouring the halls before picking my first target: Britney Nelson, a new sophomore at our school, who didn't have a lot of friends yet. However, she was cute and seemed pretty nice. I figured it shouldn't be too hard to find her a date, especially with the help of some cupid magic.

I knew who Britney was because of gym class, but we weren't close friends, so it made her the perfect choice for my first "cast the net wide" match. I could test out my cupid powers on her without being biased. I needed total objectivity to try this stuff out.

From scrutinizing her in the hall and oh so subtly peeking in her locker while she was moving stuff in and out, I'd already figured out a few key things to start her profile:

Name: Britney Nelson

Age: 16ish?

Pets: Dog, as evidenced by short, wiry hairs on her black pants. Either that, or has really hairy legs. I choose to go with the first option.

Interests: Robert Pattinson—his picture's plastered all over locker. Also loves the color pink.

Style: Girly, but casual

By examining the evidence, I'd come to the conclusion that Britney's a girl who needs a sensitive guy, one who will appreciate her femininity.

Now, to find a match for her. Eyes still on my PDA, I stepped into the line of hallway traffic.

A hard shoulder slammed into my back, and my lunch flew out of my hands. A strong, tanned hand darted out, grabbing the bag just before it hit the floor. Luckily, I kept my grip on the cupid device. Janet would so not be thrilled if I broke it on my very first day.

"Sorry," a deep voice behind me said. "Are you okay? I didn't see you."

With fumbling fingers, I pocketed the PDA, then turned around to gaze up into piercing green eyes. Derek's eyes.

"I—I, yes, I'm fine. Thanks." A slow burn crawled up my throat and across my cheeks.

He frowned, a crease between his dark blond eyebrows. "You're . . . Andy, right?"

I bit back a sigh, trying not to rub my sore shoulder. "No, I'm Felicity. Andy's friend."

He nodded, giving me a wry grin. "Oh, sorry. I always see you two together. I'm easily confused, ya know. Football and all that—probably knocked some brain cells out." He paused. "Aren't you in art class with me too? I never hear you talk in there."

He'd noticed me? I perked up. "Yup, that's me. Quiet as a mouse." And übercliché, too. *Ugh, why do I say these stupid things?*

"I'm Derek." He handed me my bag with a smile. "Okay, see you later."

"Bye." I waved at his retreating back. Oh my God, I couldn't wait to tell Andy and Maya.

In the cafeteria, I settled at my regular table beside Andy and Maya, unwrapped my turkey sandwich, and tried to refocus. Okay, back to business. I needed to match Britney up with someone. But who?

The question stuck with me throughout lunch, though I tried to act like everything was normal. Andy, in between bites of pizza, talked to me and Maya about some jerk in her homeroom who broke up with his girlfriend by having his friend dump her. So not cool. But even though I nodded and rolled my eyes and said "what a loser" at all the right parts of the story, I was only half listening. My brain was focused on cupid business.

I was tempted to ask Andy and Maya who Britney should

date, or to pry them for info that I could add to her profile, but Janet's rules kind of scared me. I was better off trying to figure this out myself.

I finished my sandwich and balled up the trash, proud of myself for not breaking down and getting a slice of pepperoni-laden pizza. As tasty as Andy's lunch had looked, I didn't need a greasy skin breakout, since junior prom was coming up soon. Of course, I didn't have a date, but neither did Andy or Maya, so I figured we could always go as a group.

While the girls kept chatting, I wandered over to the trash cans to pitch my garbage. My heart fluttered when I thought about how romantic it would be to dance with Derek at prom, even just once. I'd be sitting at the table with Maya and Andy, telling them a funny and clever story, and he'd walk up to me, a shy smile on his face, and say—

"Hey, don't throw that can away. You can recycle it."

I jumped, startled out of my daydream. "Huh?"

Matthew Cornwall, a guy from my biology class, pointed to the empty soda can in my hand. "There's a recycling bin by the front doors."

"Oh, right."

He smiled. "Thanks. Sorry to scare you. Just trying to do my part, you know." He walked away, waving hi to another guy and starting up some conversation.

Hm. Matthew seemed pretty decent—he knew how to apologize, after all. Plus, he wasn't a total jerk in class and usually had smart commentary on the lessons . . . and caring for the environment was a good quality too. Maybe he'd make a good match for Britney.

When I got back to the lunch table, I told the girls I'd meet them after school as usual, then headed over to where Matthew was talking and squatted at a nearby table, trying to look casual while eavesdropping like mad.

I turned on the PDA and created a new profile.

Name: Matthew Cornwall

Age: 17

Pets: Has a bird. Remember him talking about it in biology.

Interests: Recycling, obviously

Style: Tree-hugger

But what else?

I leaned my ear in his direction as he talked to the other guy.

For a few minutes they did nothing but go on and on about school sports. I added that to his interests list and tried not to die of boredom as they argued the finer points of one of our basketball players' stats. Then, a perfect tidbit came up.

"Hey, did you catch the opening band at Peabody's last Friday? They were awesome." Matthew grabbed a folded piece of paper out of his messenger bag and handed it to his friend. "Here's their flyer. My cousin knows the lead singer. They're playing again next month. You should go."

"Thanks, I'll try," the guy replied, stuffing the flyer in his back pocket.

Aha, so Matthew likes indie music. Peabody's is well-known in downtown Cleveland for featuring small local bands, and it was obvious from the enthusiasm in Matthew's voice that he enjoys going there.

Indie rockers are sensitive, always crying about something or another, aren't they? I went to Britney's profile, looking over what I'd found about her. Both she and Matthew have animals, and it's a well-known fact that pet people tend to like other pet people. And I was guessing that they're both the sensitive type. But what would be my third minimum trait?

Hm. They both attended Greenville High, so that could count as one common interest, couldn't it? Well, I'd make it count. Besides, after they got together, I was sure they'd find lots more in common.

Yup, it was time to do a little matchmaking.

Using the PDA, I created a blank e-mail to Britney and carbon-copied Matt.

My stomach flipped in nervousness. Before I could talk myself out of it, I hit send.

My first love match—signed, sealed, and e-mailed.

Chapter 3

TGIF! Friday is our weekly sleepover night, and I was currently perched over the edge of Andy's queen-size bed as I painted my toenails Slutty Red. That wasn't the "official" name, but whatever.

"Okay, so dish, ladies," Andy said, rubbing the green tea mask—oops, sorry, *masque*—on her face. "Whaddaya think of that Britney girl who Matthew's suddenly dating? I mean, I never even saw them talk before, and now they're practically dry humping in the hallway? What's up with that?"

I stifled a giggle at Andy's vivid but accurate description of my successful love match. Now that I was a bona fide cupid, I wasn't even grossed out by couples' smooshed-against-the-lockers Public Displays of Affection. Matthew and Britney had been locked at the lips ever since I sent the e-mail, and I couldn't have been happier about the match.

"I think it's gross," Maya said, her nose wrinkled. She pulled her long, dark hair into her trademark ponytail, grimacing at her reflection in the hand-held mirror.

"You would," Andy teased.

Maya stuck her tongue out at Andy. After dabbing clumps of masque all over her thin, pale face, she continued. "Well, who wants to see people groping like that? Get a room. I'd rather be with a guy who knows how to act like a gentleman." She paused. "Though at least Britney and Matthew seem to really like each other. They've both been beaming all week. What do you think, Felicity?"

I swallowed, suddenly nervous. As much as I wanted to 'fess up, I had to play surprised. Which meant lying to my best friends—not a fun task. I was a terrible liar, and I knew they would see right through me.

"Oh, yeah. I thought it was weird too," I said, trying to play it cool, even though my hand was shaking. "But definitely great for them."

Damn, I messed up my pinkie toenail. A big glob of Slutty Red clumped on the toe knuckle. "Hey, I need the nail polish remover."

Luckily, my friends were both too caught up in beautifying

themselves to notice my fibbing. Andy tossed me the bottle with the tips of her fingers, trying not to get green tea masque all over the cap. "Here ya go."

"Thanks. Well," I said casually, "you never know when love will strike."

Maya shot me a weird look. "Speaking of, what's going on with your job? Have you started yet?"

"Yeah." Quickly, I brought into my mind the story I'd rehearsed. "It's a lot of paperwork so far, but I've been learning the fine art of matching profiles by observing some of the pros."

In a way, that was true. I'd rented some older movies, like *Clueless*, *Emma*, and *The Wedding Planner*, to put me in the right frame of mind and maybe give me some ideas.

Maya nodded thoughtfully. "Well, maybe once you're there for a while, you'll move up and get to do some of the good stuff." She grabbed a washcloth and headed into Andy's bathroom. Yet another reason to be jealous of Andy—she had a full bathroom attached to her room, including a luxurious, claw-footed tub.

My mom wouldn't even let me keep my curling iron in our family bathroom, since she said it junked it up. However, lucky Andy's girly stuff was strewn all across hers.

"That sounds cool," Andy said. "So much better than my stupid job." She hustled into the bathroom to rinse the masque off her face, as well.

That was one thing about Andy I actually didn't envy: her job. She works as a waitress at The Burger Butler, one of those cutesy, gimmicky restaurants with a franchise in every big city. Unfortunately, she has to wear a butler uniform when she serves her customers, right down to the white gloves and bow tie. God only knows how many times she's gotten called "Jeeves" on a daily basis or had her tuxedoed butt grabbed by some pervy old man. She doesn't have to work—her parents are happy to buy her whatever she wants—but it's important to Andy to be independent and more self-reliant.

"Yeah, but at least you get free food," I pointed out.

"Like I want more burgers," Andy said, coming out of the bathroom and patting her face dry with a plush purple towel. "Besides, do you know how bad all that grease is for your complexion? I don't need any more breakouts."

"Please. You hardly need to worry about it." I finished up my toenails. There—picture-perfect. Too bad Derek would never see them. "You have gorgeous skin. Besides, your booty alone is the ultimate guy magnet."

"If all it takes to get a boyfriend is a big booty, then guys should be knocking down my front door," Maya said, coming out of the bathroom and flopping on the floor. "But they'd have to notice me first. I'm just way too nervous to talk to them the way Andy does."

Oh. My. *God.* I just got the best idea in the world. I could find a love match for Maya! Why didn't I think of that before?

Maya needed an ego boost, stat, and I had just the magic to make her dreams come true. Besides, it would be way more fun and fulfilling for me than pairing off people I don't know very well.

This was a seriously good use of my new cupid powers. Why shouldn't my friend have a great boyfriend? If I couldn't date Derek, at least Maya could be happy. I'd just have to live vicariously through her love life.

"So, Maya," I said as nonchalantly as possible, screwing the nail polish lid tightly closed, "what kind of guy are you looking for? I mean, obviously you want someone who appreciates junk in the trunk."

Maya laughed, stretching her legs out and flexing her toes. "Well, I want a smart guy who's involved in school activities, like I am. I want someone who respects me and doesn't just think about how to get in my pants. Someone who likes to have fun. And someone who isn't too macho to hang with me, or to call me to talk."

Andy snickered. "So basically, you want Prince Charming."

"Well, I guess having a white horse would be a bonus too." Maya laughed again and flung the towel at her. "Smart-ass."

"Pass the potatoes, please," Rob said, "or I'll have to arrest you for resisting an officer."

My dad chuckled, handing him the bowl of garlic mashed potatoes. "Funny."

So not funny. Rob always cracks way too many stupid cop jokes every time he comes over. My mom insists on my brother joining us every Sunday for family dinner. She says our family needs to keep in constant contact in order to stay close. I guess it's a carryover from her large Italian family.

Frankly, I think I'd feel closer to Rob if he'd stay farther away.

Rob had brought a new "flavor of the week" with him, some fake-blond chick with poofy hair and a poofier chest. I don't know where he finds these girls, but this one looked like maybe he'd picked her up for prostitution on the way here and decided to bring her to dinner instead of to jail.

Blondie giggled. "Oh, Robbie, you're too cute." She swatted his arm with her long, acrylic nails painted neon pink with tiny crystal jewels on the tips.

I think I just threw up a little in my mouth. "Hey, *Robbie*, can you pass the dinner rolls over here?"

Rob shot me a glare. "Here." He tossed me the bread basket and kicked me under the table.

"Mom," I whined, ducking a hand under the table to rub my sore shin, "call the child-abuse hotline. I'm being beaten up by my own brother. And a cop, too. For shame—always sad when the good ones turn bad like that."

This time, *she* gave me the evil eye. I shut my mouth. Some people just don't appreciate genuine humor.

"So," Mom said, turning her attention to Fluffykins, or whatever her name was (I didn't bother to learn them anymore, since women came and went out of my brother's life with alarming speed), "Where did you say you and Rob met?"

"We met on LoveMatesForever.com," she said around a spoonful of mashed potatoes. "I thought he was so dreamy. Plus, he wasn't, like, forty or anything. I'm sooooooo tired of those old guys hitting on me."

My dad nearly choked on his bread roll. I bit back a laugh. *Nice job, dumb-ass.* In one fell swoop she'd insulted both my parents, who were in their early forties.

Hey, if things didn't work out for Rob and Fluffykins—and that was a sure bet, because things *never* worked out for him—maybe I could use my matchmaking skills to find him a real girlfriend. But then I'd have to get close enough to him to observe him, and that would seriously bite. There are only so many times a day a girl can be called "butthead" by her brother before wanting to kick him in the joeys.

"Did you know Felicity works for a matchmaking company?" my mom said, trying hard to keep her polite smile in place.

Oh, crap. I should have seen that one coming.

"No way!" Bleach Blonde squealed, her bright red lips flying open. "Which one? I've joined, like, every one out there."

Rob shifted in his seat. I guess I'd feel uncomfortable too, if my date continued with the rampant stupidity.

"Well, it's a little one," I replied. "I doubt you've heard of it. I just started, so I'm not doing any of the good stuff yet. Mostly paperwork."

She squinted her heavily lined eyes at me. "Try me."

"Cupid's Hollow."

"Oh." She scooped another pile of potatoes on her fork. "Never heard of it." After chewing a bite, she glanced at Rob, then patted his hand. "Guess I don't need to worry about that now, do I, Snookie?" *Giggle, giggle.*

I shoveled the rest of my dinner down fast. I had to get out of there, now. "Excuse me," I said, carrying my plate into the kitchen before anyone could beckon me back. "Gotta go do some homework."

That was one good thing about still being in school—I always had homework to serve as a ready-made excuse for getting out of crappy family events.

Up in my room, I picked up the PDA and flipped through the many, many entries I'd made yesterday, trying to find the perfect match for Maya. There were a few candidates who seemed good and who met the minimum-compatibility requirements, but I still wasn't sure who to choose. I resolved to follow the top candidates around for a day so I could observe them as much as possible and find the perfect one.

After all, we weren't talking about any old target here. This was one of my best friends!

• • •

Monday morning, I was rarin' to go. The first thing I did after stepping inside the front doors of Greenville High was flip on my PDA and run through the entire male population of the junior and senior classes about a billion times. After much scrutiny, I finally narrowed the candidates for Maya down to three possibilities: Josh Wiley, the drum major of the band; Ben Johnson, the announcer for the school's basketball games; and Quentin Lovejoy, the editor in chief of the yearbook.

All three of those guys were highly involved in school activities, one of Maya's big criteria, and just as importantly, I'd never heard complaints from other girls about them being total buttheads. Plus, they were all cute and smart, so putting them at the top of the lineup made total sense.

Therefore, my mission was to pay special attention to these three lead candidates for Operation Hook Maya Up and determine who was most worthy of my friend's affection.

As I gathered further profile data throughout the day, watching the guys closely, my initial thoughts were confirmed. All three would be great for Maya. The more I observed of the three of them, the harder it was to choose among them.

In art class, my last class of the day, I sat in the back corner, doodling absentmindedly on the corner of my latest project, a pencil sketch of a pile of books. I was too wrapped up in matchmaking Maya to even stare at Derek's gorgeous face from under the shield of my eyelashes, like I normally did (although he did acknowledge me in class today with a nod and smile). I needed to figure out which guy would be the best choice for Maya, but the decision was overwhelming me.

How could I pick just one of them?

Then, still staring at the books in my drawing, I had a sudden realization. Maybe it wasn't fair of me to make the choice for her—didn't Maya have a right to choose for herself which guy she liked best? I stopped doodling and pulled out my PDA, nestling it in my lap, then turned it on and opened up the e-mail program.

I typed in Maya's e-mail address and then carbon copied Josh, Ben, *and* Quentin. Matching all of them up like this was so against the rules—but then again, didn't Janet tell me to trust my gut? Surely the "gut" clause trumped the so-called "rules"—right?

And my gut was saying loud and clear, "Hedge your bets, Felicity! Send it to them all." I mean, what are friends for?

Time for Maya, with a little help from me, to get the kind of attention she deserved. Drawing in a deep breath, I hit send.

Chapter 4

When the bell rang dismissing school for the day, I dashed to the front doors to meet Maya for our after-school study session. We were prepping for a test in first period English on *The Grapes of Wrath*. I'd actually read this one and was ready to go, though the ending grossed me out.

Breast-feeding an old guy? Nasty. Who decided to make *that* a classic?

Andy, who was outside yapping with Maya, wasn't going to get her nerd groove on with the two of us, since she wasn't in me and Maya's English class. However, it was tradition for the three of us to walk home together.

We headed down the icy sidewalk. Luckily, Maya's house was only a few blocks away. In thin pants, I was freezing my buns off. I rubbed my hands together, then crammed them in my coat pockets, wishing I'd remembered my gloves.

"Did you hear?" Andy asked, shouldering her backpack a little better over her coat. Her breath huffed out in little clouds.

"Hear what?" I asked, eager for her to dish details. Andy always had the good scoop.

"Mallory Robinson was flirting way hard with Derek today at second lunch. Jenny Mack was sitting across the table from them, and she told Amanda West, who told me. Mallory's probably doing it just because she knows you like him."

My stomach clenched. "God, seriously?"

Mallory Robinson was my mortal enemy, and if there was a way for her to make my life miserable, she was after it. It looked like flirting with Derek was a new addition to her "let's torture Felicity" list.

"What are you going to do about it?" Maya asked me.

I shrugged.

"I know," Andy volunteered. "You should tell Derek you like him before that piece of trash steals him away."

Man, I wished I could. If only the cupid law was different. But I couldn't just throw some e-mail love his way and make him come running to me. And without the cupid magic, he barely knew I was alive.

"I don't know," I said. "I guess I'll figure something out."

This sucked. The one guy I'd been in love with forever was off-limits.

Or was he?

Janet had told me I couldn't matchmake myself. But that didn't mean I couldn't be available if *he* wanted to date *me*, right? If I could get him to fall for me without using the magic, it wouldn't be breaking any cupid rules.

But how on earth was I going to do that? I needed to think about this more. There had to be something I could do to make Derek notice me. If he ended up with Mallory, I swear I'd spontaneously combust.

Once Maya and I arrived at her house, we darted inside, waving bye to Andy, and ran upstairs to her bedroom. Maya hopped onto her computer to check e-mail, as usual.

However, this time was different. I'd get to watch my love match in action.

As she booted up her PC, my heart pounded, and I realized my hands were shaking slightly. What if I messed it up? What if she realized what I was doing? What if the triple-match strategy backfired, and the guys all fell for each other instead of for Maya?

I stuffed my hands in my pockets to keep from showing my nervousness. "Um . . ."

"Hold on a sec, Felicity. I got e-mail."

I sat on her bed and nodded, holding my breath for what seemed like an eternity.

Maya double-clicked with the mouse, then froze. She stared at the monitor. After a moment, she shook her head, blinking. "What were we talking about?" she asked, rubbing the middle of her chest.

It worked! She must have been feeling the same tingle I'd experienced when Janet hit me with the arrow. "Oh, you know," I said oh so casually, "just talking about guys."

She spun in her seat and looked at me, a dreamy smile on her face. It almost freaked me out—I'd never seen her look . . . blissful before. With her face so soft, she almost looked like a different person.

"You know who I like?" She sighed, putting her hand to her heart. "Josh Wiley, Ben Johnson, and Quentin Lovejoy."

Bingo.

That afternoon, after studying with Maya and running home quickly to change clothes, I bummed Mom's car and made my way to Cupid's

Hollow headquarters, where I was scheduled for my first one-on-one meeting with my boss to discuss the state of my cupid affairs for the week.

Janet had been pretty friendly during my interview and training session, but now that I was a true employee, I quickly found out that she could be plenty intimidating when she wanted to. She sat at her desk like a dictator at a podium, peering down her nose at me. Or maybe she just seemed extra scary since I was terrified I'd get fired for having already broken a rule in my first week on the job.

Trying to remain as calm and professional as possible, I filled her in on my pair-ups for Britney and Maya, using generic statements for Maya's match and carefully omitting the part about having carbon-copied all three guys.

With a brisk nod, Janet said, "Sounds like you've done a good job so far, Felicity." She wrote a note in her ever-present notebook. "So, you made one match last week and one this week. Way to go."

I shifted in my seat. Nervous as hell, I'd dressed to impress in my best outfit—a semisheer white blouse, lacy white tank top, and deep blue A-line skirt. Unfortunately, the skirt was also made of the itchiest fabric known to mankind.

I'd bought it because it was super cute, but every time I wore it,

I ended up scratching myself like I had fleas. Not very attractive.

"Thanks," I said to Janet. "It's been fun so far."

"Well, why don't you hand over your LoveLine 3000 so I can upload your information into the main computer. I can also port updated e-mail addresses to you this way."

At her words, my heart stopped beating and nearly jumped out of my chest. I hadn't realized she'd actually want to *see* the matches. If I handed her the PDA, she'd know instantly that I'd matched Maya up with three guys, thus breaking a cupid rule. Would she buy my "gut" reasoning?

Instinct told me not to find out.

"I'm sorry, I left it at home," I said, pasting on a huge, fake smile. With my heel, I subtly nudged my purse—the one that currently held said PDA—under my chair. "That was so stupid of me. I can bring it in next time, though. Will that work?"

"Sure," she replied, "but please bring it in then." She glanced at her watch. "Okay, you're free to go. I'll see you next Monday."

Sweet, blissful relief surged through my limbs. Thank God I'd have time to delete Maya's match and claim it was an "accident."

I stood and shook her hand. "You got it!"

"If you feel comfortable with it," she said as I slid my arms into my coat, "try upping your quota to two matches this week."

I nodded. "Absolutely. I can do that."

"Oh, wait." She flipped through a manila folder on her desk, then handed me a check. "Here you go. I'll be paying you weekly at our meetings."

I grinned widely. "Thanks!" *Sweet!* It wasn't a land mine, but I'd earned this paycheck. And I was doubly happy to find out I'd be getting paid weekly.

After the meeting, I hopped in Mom's Camry and pulled out of the parking lot, giddy with relief. I'd managed to avert certain disaster and keep my awesome job. Janet had praised my matches and even upped my quota. And tomorrow, I'd get to witness the biggest payoff of all.

Boy, would Maya be surprised when the three guys started wooing her! I couldn't wait to see her happy face.

I was seriously the best friend ever. Of course, Maya would never know I was the reason for her dating surge, but that didn't matter. It would be my little anonymous contribution to the whole "pay it forward" concept.

About a mile from my house, I shifted the car into the right lane. Suddenly, a wailing siren appeared from out of nowhere behind me, and blue and red lights flashed in my rearview mirror.

But I wasn't speeding or anything! And I'd even used my turn signal (which I freely admit, I sometimes forget about). Crap, I was in serious trouble now. Mom would kill me for getting a ticket while driving her car.

"Pull over!" a loud voice barked over the police car's megaphone.

With shaky hands, I sucked in shallow breaths and did as instructed, parking on the side of the road. I dug into my purse to find my license, barely able to concentrate. I was in such deep sh—

The megaphone interrupted my thoughts. "Ma'am, we know you're using the marijuana!"

I clenched my jaw. I'd know that irritating voice from anywhere.

Pissed off, I hopped out of the car, stomped to my brother's cop car, and stood by his door, hands on hips. I cussed loudly, scaring an old lady crossing the street. She blinked at me and walked faster, trying to get away from me.

"Geez, Rob, you scared the piss out of me!" I yelled. "I thought I was in real trouble. You're such a jerk."

Rob and his partner were in the front seat, bent over laughing. Rob straightened, then said through the megaphone, "Stop cussing at me or I'm going to have to take you in."

I shot him the most evil glare I could muster. "Stop pulling me over!" I shouted at him through the window. "This is the second time now you've done this to me. It's still not funny."

He rolled down his window and stuck his head out. "Then, ma'am, stop driving in this city."

"But I live here!" I turned on my heel and headed back to the car.

"And, ma'am," Rob hollered to my back, his voice ringing loud and clear throughout all of Cleveland, no doubt, "lay off the spray tan! Your skin's starting to look orange."

I whirled back around and stomped toward him, unable to control my rage. "If you pull me over again," I said, pointing my finger in his face, "I'll tell Mom about the time I caught you making out with Cindy Masterson in Mom and Dad's bed when you two were supposed to be studying."

His jaw dropped. He tried to cover up his fear, but I could see it in his eyes. "You wouldn't."

I leaned close to his face, then widened my eyes and blinked rapidly, gasping. "Mom, it was awful! He was touching her under her shirt! I didn't know *what* to do!"

Rob stared at me for a long moment, then tipped his hat. "Have a nice day." He drove off in a hurry.

Chapter 5

Tuesday morning, I walked with Maya to school, shuffling carefully along the slick, snow-encrusted sidewalks. Sooty gray clouds hung low in the air. *Great*—more snow was surely coming. Cleveland in March sucked hard. But my thoughts were quickly taken off the weather and returned to the huge success that was Operation Hook Maya Up.

Case in point: Josh, the drum major, was already waiting outside the front doors, his gaze scouring the grounds. When he saw me and Maya walk up the front steps, he waved, his breath coming out in rapid puffs at the sight of her.

"Hiya, Maya," Josh said, a smile plastered across his face. It was dorky, for sure, but still pretty darn cute. Bright pink spots tinged his cheeks and the tips of his ears, and I wondered if it was from the cold or from the excitement of seeing Maya. "Need help with your backpack or trumpet case or anything?"

Without waiting for an answer, he snagged both items in question. His body now laden with an instrument case and two backpacks, he looked like a lovesick bellhop.

"Oh, hey, Josh," Maya said, her lips wavering in a small, surprised smile. "Thanks for the help." She snuggled deeper into her thick black coat.

This was definitely friendlier and less tongue-tied than Maya normally was around guys, but she didn't seem as head over heels for Josh as he was for her. Interesting. Given the way the magic had worked with Britney and Matthew, I'd half expected Maya and Josh to be playing tonsil hockey by now.

Maya headed up the steps, and Josh teetered by her side, ignoring me completely.

"Oh, hey," I mumbled to Josh's back, a little miffed that he couldn't even bother to say hi or acknowledge my existence. "No, I'm fine, thanks for asking."

"Do you always talk to yourself?" a guy's voice said.

I turned gingerly to my right, trying not to slip on any icy patches lingering on the school steps. It was Derek, leaning against the concrete stair ramp, bearing a deep smirk as he looked at me.

My heart did that funky pitter-patter it always does when I see him. "Oh, h-hi." Gee, stuttering is sexy. My oh so witty reply was sure to dazzle him.

Derek slid up beside me, and we headed into the building like everything was normal. As if we did this all the time. I felt like everyone's eyes were on me, though in reality, no one probably gave a crap about me and who I walked with.

I looked for Maya among the clusters tromping through the hallway, but she was already out of my sight. I hoped everything was going okay with her and Josh. Luckily, I'd have a chance to talk to her in our first-period English class, as well as at lunch. That is, if I managed not to pass out from forgetting how to breathe, due to the distraction of Derek's incredible hotness by my side.

"Well, see ya," Derek said, taking off down the hallway to the left.

"Okay," I croaked, waving bye to him with waggly fingers. I headed to my locker. Damn, I should have had something more clever to say than "huh-hi," or "okay." *Stupid Felicity.* This was not the way to get his attention. I grabbed my books from my locker and took off for English.

Maya was already in the classroom, sitting straight up in her seat.

She waved me over beside her, eyes wide, mouth shaped like an O.

"You won't believe what just happened," she breathed. "Josh asked me out. On a date. For tonight! Can you believe it? He's so sweet."

At least someone's love life was going the right way. "That's awesome," I said, pushing my own Derek woes out of my mind. I had a job to do, and Maya was a part of that. Plus, I was utterly thrilled for my friend and wanted to make sure she knew how excited I was. *Focus.* "What kind of date?"

"He wants to take me to dinner and a movie. I think we're going to go see—"

"Shh," Mrs. Kendel interrupted, the permanent scowl deepening on her face. I turned away from Maya and faced forward in my seat. Our teacher was not a good person to piss off.

Mrs. Kendel handed out the *Grapes of Wrath* test to every student, the gold bangles on her right wrist clanging with the repetitive motion. "It's time to pay attention. This is not an open-book or open-note test. You have thirty minutes to complete the exam. Please use a number-two pencil and write legibly in the short-answer portion. You may beginnnnnn . . ." she drawled off, staring at her thin gold watch in silence for several seconds. "Now."

As I read the first question and filled in my answer, I glanced at

Maya from the corner of my eye (no, I wasn't cheating). I took in her faded jeans and black sweater, her pale, unmade face, and her dark hair tied back with a black ponytail holder. I swear, Maya's wardrobe was filled with so much black, Death himself had to be jealous. I tried to observe her with an unbiased point of view, to see her not as a best friend, but as a professional cupid.

Hm, if one of these love matches was going to last past the two-week love-glow period, which would be a total win-win for everyone involved, we were gonna have to do some makeover changes, stat. Maybe during lunch we could do some wardrobe replanning, and this weekend, I could take her to get her hair cut and highlighted—

A knock on the classroom door startled us all. I looked up and saw a guy peering through the glass panel, scanning the room. It was Quentin, the yearbook editor and love match #2 for Maya. His eyes lit up when he saw her beside me.

"Mr. Lovejoy," Mrs. Kendel said, ripping the door open with a meaty hand, "can we help you, sir? We're in the middle of a test."

"Sorry, Mrs. Kendel," Quentin said, unable to tear his eyes from Maya, "but this couldn't wait." He stepped past the teacher and crossed the room, stopping in front of Maya. He took her hand in his, then dropped down on one knee, tugging a folded piece of paper out of his back pocket with his free hand. "I wrote a poem for you, Maya. It took me all night to compose it."

Maya's jaw, along with every other jaw in the classroom, hung open. "You did? For me?" she pulled it together to ask.

"Mr. Lovejoy, we don't have time for this nonsense," Mrs. Kendel said. She opened the door wider. "You need to leave."

"But if I don't get to read my poem, my heart will die," Quentin said, swallowing hard. I'd never seen a guy that serious about love in my life. "It'll only take a minute. Please."

"Come on," one of the girls in class said. "Let him read the poem!"

"Yeah," others started chiming in. "Let him read!"

"Zip it!" Mrs. Kendel barked to the class. She looked at Quentin. "You have thirty seconds, starting now."

"Thank you!" He looked at his paper and began to read, pouring emotion into his voice. "Ode to Maya." He paused dramatically. "The sun rises and sets in your fair face. Being near you makes my heart race. Your laughter, wit, and style are so bright, I'd love to take you out tonight."

Oh, God. That was the cheesiest thing I'd ever heard in my life. It took him all night to write that? I'd hate to see the first few drafts of that puppy.

Apparently, the guys in the class agreed with me, judging from their loud guffaws. "Way to go, lover boy," one ribbed. "That'll get you laid for sure."

"Hush, Mr. Packard," Mrs. Kendel snapped.

Tom Packard's girlfriend elbowed him in the side, and he grunted loudly.

"Shut up, you jerk," she cried, her voice thin and watery. "That was the most romantic thing I've ever seen. How come you never write *me* poems?"

Quentin ignored them both, focusing solely on Maya's ever-reddening face.

"Say yes!" someone shouted.

"Yes, yes, yes!" girls chanted.

Blinking rapidly, Maya nodded, smiling. "Sure, that sounds good."

The class broke out in applause. You'd think he'd just proposed to her, the way he jumped up and hugged her, almost knocking her out of her chair.

"Well, now that that's finished, you can leave, Mr. Lovejoy," Mrs. Kendel said, attempting to regain her control of the classroom. But even she looked moved by the gesture. Who would have thought beneath that withered skin of hers beat the heart of a romantic?

With one last wink, Quentin slipped out the door, a modern-day Romeo who had likely just won the heart of every girl in class, and turned Maya into an instant celeb.

I stared at the closed door, stunned. Wow. This cupid thing was way more powerful than I'd realized. I tried to go back to focusing on my English test, but really, who could concentrate after a display like that?

One thing was for sure: Quentin and Josh had it bad for Maya, even worse than she seemed to have it for them. And given the pattern, I'd be willing to bet that Ben, the third match, would be the same way.

Now I could see why Janet had discouraged group matches like this. It seemed the guys' love was much stronger than Maya's, since it was aimed only at her, but her love was weaker since it was divided among the three of them.

Maybe that wasn't such a bad thing, though. At least Maya would be in her right mind when all three of them tried to date her.

I scrawled out the short answers on my test with a half-assed effort, not caring at the moment about the woes of the Great Depression. Then, I stopped writing mid-sentence. Maya had told Josh and

Quentin she'd go on a date with each of them—tonight. Crap. So much for staying clear-headed.

When Mrs. Kendel called time, we all put our pencils down and handed our tests up the rows. I took the opportunity to lean over and talk to Maya. "Hey—isn't your date with *Josh* tonight too? You just double-booked!"

She gasped. "Oh, no. You're right! What was I thinking?" Her face fell. "I just got so excited at being asked out. And I really like them both."

I couldn't blame her. After a dating dry period of, oh, her whole life, it's no wonder she got that way. It would be like starving for sixteen years, then being taken to a buffet and getting wooed by the steaks. Or something like that. "We'll figure it out," I said.

Mrs. Kendel shot me and Maya a small glare, then went over to the chalkboard and started writing. "Okay, let's go over the test answers together."

The rest of the period flew by fast, as did the whole morning. I mostly zoned out in my classes and fretted over the Maya dilemma, not sure what to tell her. How would we figure out which guy to ditch tonight? And what would we do if Ben demanded a date with her too?

At lunch, Andy met up with us, sliding into a seat beside Maya and unwrapping her food with gusto. "Hey, girls," she said between bites of a burrito. "How are things going?"

Maya inched in close to her. "You won't believe my day!" She filled her in on the Josh-and-Quentin love-fest.

"Geez, that beats my day by far." Andy shook her head, a new admiration for Maya lighting her eyes. "What, do you have a guy magnet or something on today?"

Maya shrugged. "I don't know. Just my lucky day, I guess. Right now, though, I have to figure out which date to postpone." As she spoke, her voice wavered, and her face grew paler, if that was even possible. She slumped in her seat. "But what if I cancel with one, and he changes his mind and decides he doesn't want to see me at all?" She groaned and leaned forward, thunking her head in her hands. "I like them both! I don't want to have to choose."

"I wouldn't worry about them losing interest," I said, patting Maya on the back. "They both seemed pretty smitten." Of course, I knew she'd have two weeks of their undivided attention, but there wasn't any way I could say that without giving away trade secrets.

Andy tilted her head and twirled a strand of hair around her pinkie, considering the situation. "There's no way to know that for sure, though. Guys are so hormonal. Maybe it's better not to tempt fate."

We sat in silence for a moment. Then, Andy snapped her fingers. "I think there's only one solution, Maya—you'll go out with both of them, tonight." She looked at me, and I recognized that expression in her eyes. It was stubborn determination. "And Felicity and I will help you juggle your two dates."

Chapter 6

And that's why, on a Tuesday night, when I should have been home doing quadratic equations, or washing my hair, or anything else in the world, I was listening to my iPod and staring at the back of Josh's slightly shaggy head of hair in the darkened movie theater. He'd just crammed another fistful of popcorn into his mouth, nodding in enthusiasm as blood spurted from a severed arm on the screen.

Ew. I popped a Whopper in my mouth and sucked on the chocolaty coating, reveling in the taste. I couldn't believe I'd agreed to this scheme, but Andy had worked her magic over lunch and talked me into it. I'd even pointed out to her and Maya that things like this never worked right except in the movies, but Andy was convinced we could pull it off.

Besides, Maya had looked so hopeful about the idea, I just couldn't say no. This was, after all, sorta kinda partially my fault, if only in a strictly technical and by-the-book kind of way. I'd broken a cupid rule, so I had to help clean up the mess.

Well, at least I wasn't the only one on recon duty. Andy was doing the exact same thing with Quentin in the next theater over. We'd agreed beforehand to stick to the guys like white on rice while Maya bounced back and forth between them.

The girl in the seat beside me elbowed me in the arm for the four hundredth time, and I shot her an evil glare, trying to reclaim my armrest. Not that she was paying any attention to me, since she was too busy cramming her tongue in her guy's ear.

Which I normally wouldn't care about, if she weren't making revolting slurping sounds every time. *Slurp slurp. Giggle giggle. Slurp slurp.* It was disgusting.

I cranked up the sound on my iPod and sank into my seat, two rows back from my target. Josh had taken Maya to the six thirty showing of *He Knows Who You Are*. It was a horror piece of B-grade crap starring some fluffball Hollywood hoochie of the month. This actress couldn't do a scene without either losing an article of clothing or tripping over a blade of grass as she screamed in overexaggerated fright.

The movie was cheesy, and a bit on the gory side, with limbs being hacked off left and right. Totally not my thing. So I entertained myself with my iPod on shuffle and kept my eyes carefully trained on Josh.

Not that he'd moved from his seat. He was an easygoing date, for sure. In the forty minutes we'd been in the theater, Maya had already excused herself twice, as we'd planned. Before the dates, Andy had mapped out a route plan and time-share schedule, and the three of us had come up with a whole list of reasons for her to sneak out of the theaters.

We'd also decided Maya would have coffee with Quentin before their movie and go into the theater with him. And then, right before the other movie would start, she'd duck out to meet Josh and head into *their* theater together, alternating back and forth at regular intervals during the flicks. At the end of the movies, she'd tell Quentin good night and have dessert with Josh afterward. Equal time for equal dates.

I had to hand it to Andy, she was unbelievably good at scheming. The master planner, indeed. If I ever got in a situation where I had to date two guys at the same time, I knew who to go to.

Yeah, right. Like that would happen.

I took a sip of my Coke, downed another couple of delicious Whoppers, then skipped to a more upbeat song to tune out the stupid actress's piercing scream in the movie.

Forty-three minutes in, and it was Maya's turn to be with Josh again. She was leaning into his side, whispering something in his ear. His shoulders shook as he laughed at whatever she said, and then he reached an arm over and wrapped it around her, tugging her closer.

A lump clogged my throat as I watched them. I was both happy for Maya and a little sad for myself. It was a bittersweet feeling knowing I was helping her find love but not being able to do a darn thing about my own pathetic love life.

Plus, I felt really bizarre watching them, like I was some kind of pervert. I mean, what kind of person goes to the movies alone and watches couples like this? Lonely old men? Yeah, it was the good-friend thing to do, but this was still a bit awkward.

I'd damn well better get some Twizzlers out of it, at least. I wished for the ten billionth time that year that I owned a cell phone. Then at least I could text Andy to see how things were going on her side.

After another few minutes of watching the movie, Maya said

something to Josh, then crouched and hustled her way out of her row, slipping down the steps and out of the theater. Josh leaned back in his seat and took a draw from the ginormous Styrofoam cup, focusing on the film.

I wonder, what excuse did she use this time? Phone call from her mom? Soda spilled on her shirt? More popcorn? A pee break? And how many excuses had she burned through by now? We still had an hour left in the movie, and I didn't want her to run out.

I looked down at my iPod and scrolled through the albums. Who did I want to listen to now? Maybe I'd play some old music. I had the *Grease* sound track in there, which I'd snagged from my mom's collection and uploaded on a whim. I clicked it, listening in amusement to John Travolta and Olivia Newton-John croon about summer lovin'. Maybe in a few months I'd have my own summer love—preferably one named Derek.

Another scream ripped through the theater, and I jerked slightly in my seat in shock, looking up at the screen. The hoochie was lying on a bed, strategically covering her surgically enhanced, heaving bare chest with her perfectly manicured hands as some guy in a black trench coat stalked closer and closer, leering in anticipation. I love Maya, but she truly has terrible taste in movies.

I glanced down at Josh to see his reaction . . . but he wasn't there.

My heart stopped beating for a second, then slammed hard in my chest. Oh God, where was he?

Leaning forward in my seat, I scoured the dark theater as best as possible. Josh was nowhere to be found. He must have slipped out when I was daydreaming about Derek.

Crap!

Way to go, Felicity. I had one job tonight, to keep an eye on Josh, and I'd already blown it.

I yanked out my earbuds and crammed the iPod in my pocket. Time to get out of there and find Josh . . . before he could find Maya with Quentin.

Okay, calm down. I forced myself to take several deep breaths. He was probably just getting a reload of popcorn, or something like that. Maya and Quentin were safely in another theater, and Josh would have no possible reason to go in there. Maya wasn't scheduled to emerge from the other movie for at least five more minutes. Nothing was going to go wrong.

I rose from my seat and tripped over the legs of the make-out slurper beside me.

"Excuse me," I mumbled, not bothering to wait for a response. I headed to the end of the aisle, then ran down the stairs and out of the room.

The lobby was bustling with people shuffling through lines to get popcorn, tugging children's hands to keep them from disappearing. I saw three shaggy-haired guys horsing around near a coming attractions cardboard cutout, and a guy I recognized from the basketball team on a date with a redheaded cheerleader. But no Josh.

Where could he be?

A hand clamped down on my shoulder. Heart in throat, I spun around. It was Andy, and she looked unusually freaked out, her breath coming out in short bursts. She tucked a strand of hair behind her ear. "There you are!" she said. "Josh just went in the bathroom!"

I heaved a huge sigh of relief. "Oh, thank God. I thought I'd—"

"Quentin's in there already, *and he just finished a jumbo Coke*!" she blurted.

Oh, no. No doubt they'd see each other in there. After all, guys don't pee in individual stalls like girls do, do they? No, they have those urinal thingies they line up against.

And if they saw each other—I mean, if they saw each other's face, not their guy parts—they'd probably start talking . . . and then, they'd surely find out both of them were on a date with the same girl.

"Where's Maya?" I asked, trying to keep control over my shaking voice.

"She's still in the movie. We gotta do something, now." Andy's hand clutched my shoulder harder, her fingers digging under the bone.

I flinched under her killer grip. "Hey, that hurts. Okay, okay, I'll fix this."

I eyed the men's restroom, and a sick thud of realization hit the bottom of my stomach. There was only one way to keep this thing from escalating.

Drawing in a deep breath and screwing up my courage, I marched straight ahead and pushed the men's bathroom door open with a mighty heave.

"Oh, man!" I squealed as I rushed in. "I gotta pee like crazy!"

I froze dead in my tracks. The row of men all lined up in front of the urinals turned, wide-eyed, and stared at me in shock.

Including Quentin and Josh. They were standing right beside

each other. Neither one was throwing punches, so I must have burst in on time.

"Aaaaaah!" Quentin gasped when he saw me, turning away from me to zip his pants. His hands moved so fast, I hoped he wouldn't accidentally catch "it" in the zipper.

"Felicity?" Josh said in a horrified tone, then followed Quentin's lead quickly when he realized I could almost see his junk. "What are you—"

"Omigodthisisn'tthewomen'sbathroom!" I blurted in a rush, my words tripping over each other. I didn't have to fake the nervous edge in my voice. "I'm so sorry!"

Urinus interruptus accomplished, I backed out of the bathroom and let the door swing shut behind me, then plopped with shaky legs down on the bench against the wall, right beside Andy. That was quite possibly the weirdest, nastiest experience of my life, and I wanted to take a super-hot shower to scrub off the dirty feeling.

"Did you get there in time?" Andy asked. "What were they doing?"

As if in answer to her question, Quentin and Josh both rushed out of the bathroom, almost running in the opposite directions to their respective theaters.

With a visible sigh of relief, Andy nodded at me in approval, a smirk curling the corner of her mouth. She didn't even look surprised about my rash idea, and I wondered how many men's bathrooms she'd gone into . . . or, even worse, thought I'd been in.

"You're good," she said to me, rising from the bench. "Okay, we gotta go finish this date. We'll talk later." She took off running behind Quentin.

I took my time following Josh back to the theater—I didn't want him to think I was a stalker—and filed back toward my row, sinking deftly into my seat. Even Slurpy McGiggle's skanky make-out sound effects didn't seem as gross as what had just happened.

Pushing my earbuds back in, I turned on my iPod and waited the rest of the date out. Operation Hook Maya Up was turning out to be crazier than I'd ever imagined.

Chapter 7

The next day, I arrived at school with the furry hood of my winter coat tightly wrapped around my face so only my nose and mouth showed; I was nervous about being seen by Josh or Quentin. I just knew they thought I was some kind of bathroom peeper, and I didn't feel like facing them this morning. My only hope was that they were still so blinded by love (or so embarrassed at having been caught with their zippers down) that they wouldn't bother to mention the encounter to anyone else. That last thing I needed was for everyone at school to be laughing at my expense.

Luckily, the dates had ended well enough last night. Maya had said good night to Quentin (with a hug in the lobby) before her movie with Josh ended. She'd then headed out for post-movie dessert with Josh. Both guys had also asked Maya out again. Thankfully, instead of accepting on the spot, she'd promised to call them and set the dates up in the near future. And she was still equally smitten with them both, so it was totally worth my embarrassment to see Maya coming out of her shell like this.

I looked down the hall as I shuffled into the building and spied Maya standing frozen in front of her open locker, her jaw dropped to the floor. I hurried over, wondering what disaster had happened. Had Quentin and Josh found out about their double dates somehow and left Maya breakup notes in her locker? Or had she somehow figured out that her sudden luck with guys was due to cupid magic?

When she saw me, she grabbed my upper arm, her eyes wide and slightly buggy. "Felicity," she breathed, "you won't believe it. You know Ben? Ben Johnson?"

Oh, Ben! In all the madness with Quentin and Josh, I'd forgotten about pairing him up with Maya too. Duh!

Come to think about it, I hadn't seen him in school at all yesterday. "What about him?" I asked her.

Maya thrust a folded note into my hand. "Read this."

I unfolded the paper and read the scrawling handwriting.

Maya,

I was sick yesterday, so I didn't get to ~~see~~ talk to you, but you were all I could think about. I would like to have lunch with you today. My treat.

~~Sincer~~ Love,

Ben

"Wow, he wrote 'love,'" I said. I knew he was under the cupid spell, but I was still surprised.

"I know," she said, still breathy. "I just can't believe it. I always thought he was cute, but I didn't know he'd noticed me."

"So I take it you're saying yes?"

She took the note back and pressed it against her heart, her shiny mouth sliding into a slow smile. Wait—was Maya wearing *lip gloss*?

It was sheer, but yes, I detected a hint of glossy pink tint on her lips. And now that I was looking closer, her eyelids had a touch of light brown eye shadow on them.

"Are you wearing makeup?" I asked, dumbfounded.

She shrugged, a blush creeping across her cheeks. "Just a little. Why, does it look bad?"

She put the note in her pocket, then lifted her hand and went to wipe the gloss off her mouth.

I grabbed her arm to stop her. "No, don't do that. It looks . . . great. I was just surprised, that's all."

Even her traditional ponytail seemed a little nicer today than usual. She'd curled a few loose strands of hair around her face.

"This is crazy," Maya said, shaking her head. "I can't believe that three guys—" She jerked in surprise, then dug into her pocket. "Hold on, I think someone's texting me. Must be Andy."

She flipped her cell phone open, clicking the buttons a couple of times, and scanned the message. Then, her smile grew bigger.

"That was Quentin, thanking me for the date last night. He said he can't wait to see me today!" She closed the cell and looked at me. "This is so overwhelming. Why is this happening to me?"

Impulsively, I hugged her. "It's happening because you're an awesome person, and boys are finally starting to notice that," I said, pouring my heart into my voice.

"Well, thank you for helping me last night. You and Andy are a godsend," Maya whispered into my shoulder.

Another pair of arms wrapped around the both of us. "Hey, I wanna join the love-fest too," Andy cooed, squeezing us tightly.

We laughed.

"How come you're so late getting to school today?" I asked her. "Usually you're here before we are."

Andy grimaced and released us, rubbing the small of her back. "I'm exhausted, that's why. After I got back from Maya's dates last night, Mom made me practice yoga positions with her for an hour. I collapsed in bed without even setting my alarm. I think the dog actually woke me up."

Maya snickered, shaking her head. "Yoga, huh? Your mom is so trendy."

"Yeah, it's her new hobby of the month. She walks around in yoga pants and a tank top all day, breaking into new poses every couple of minutes. My dad is threatening to stick her out on the lawn if she doesn't stop."

We all erupted into laughter just as the first bell rang. Time to hustle. English class would wait for no man—or teen girl, in my case.

Mrs. Kendel practically pushed me and Maya in the room, then closed the door behind us.

"Ms. Takahashi," she said to Maya, looking down at her over her nose, "I trust we won't have any further disruptions in class today? No one bursting into the room bearing a Candygram, breaking into song, or other declarations of love?"

Maya shook her head and reddened slightly as the students around us tittered. She took her seat, and I sat in mine beside her, shooting her an empathetic look.

The teacher strolled up and down the aisles, handing out our next novel. *Jane Eyre*, by Charlotte Brontë.

Almost in unison, the guys in the room let out a miserable groan when they saw what we were reading.

"Come *on*," DeShawn Wallace mumbled, thumping the book down on his desk. "Can't we read something that's not a *romance*? Those are so boring. 'Oh, I love you so much, my darling!'" he said in a falsetto, batting his eyelashes.

DeShawn is the very embodiment of the quintessential arrogant, irritating male. Every time he speaks, I can't fight the massive eye-rolling.

My intense dislike of him started back in fifth grade, when he'd pantsed me in front of the class. Because of that underwear-flashing debacle, it took years for people to stop calling me "Fruit of the Loom."

So, my hackles went up instantly at DeShawn's words.

"And what's wrong with romance?" I said, unable to bite back the snippy edge in my voice. "Maybe if you read these kinds of books, you could hold on to a girlfriend for longer than a week."

Okay, that wasn't nice. I instantly felt a twinge in my stomach for being so hostile in reply. Yeah, DeShawn was a jerk, but his insult hadn't been aimed at me directly . . . just at my line of employment. Besides, he didn't know I was a cupid. I needed to stop taking him so personally. "Look, I'm sorry, but—" I started.

"Oooooooh," one of the jocks behind him interrupted me, laughing hard. He slammed a palm in DeShawn's back, shoving him forward. "Burned!"

"Zip it, everyone," Mrs. Kendel said, shooting me a quick frown, then turning her attention to DeShawn. "Mr. Wallace, if you don't care for my choice in reading material, perhaps you'd like for everyone to read *War and Peace* and write a report on it, instead."

She dug into a drawer in her desk, grabbed what was quite

possibly the biggest novel I'd ever seen, and slammed it down in front of DeShawn.

I stared in disbelief. No one else but Mrs. Kendel would threaten a sixteen-year-old that way . . . and mean it.

DeShawn's lips pinched together. He shook his head slowly. He had to be feeling the heated burn of the entire class glaring at him. *Jane Eyre* was definitely the better, quicker read, and no one wanted his big mouth to blow it for us.

"No?" Mrs. Kendel asked him, then snagged up the tome. "Then I trust we'll let me decide what's right for the class." She turned around, stuffed *War and Peace* back in her drawer, and headed for the chalkboard.

While Mrs. Kendel's chalk squeaked out biographical details about Charlotte Brontë on the board, DeShawn shot me an angry glare. Like I'd made him rant about romance. Oh well, I was disgusted with him, too. What is it with guys like that? What he needed was a good girlfriend to straighten his sorry self out.

At that moment, a beam of pure enlightenment hit me. I was totally the best person to distract DeShawn from his own obnoxiousness and help him experience true love. It was the perfect comeuppance. Mr. "Romance Sucks" was going to be the next on my list for matchmaking. He'd probably be way less annoying—and way more vulnerable—when he was head over heels for someone. And it would be highly amusing to watch him get all mushy-gushy in loooooove.

In fact, I bet he'd be desperate to pick up any tips possible on how to hang on to a girl. I could help him with that too.

I chuckled to myself and grabbed my notebook. This cupid job was full of perks I hadn't considered before. Hell, maybe I'd find matches for all the disbelievers in school, just to teach them how wrong it was to snub romance.

A pale-faced Ben was waiting for Maya outside the room, almost bouncing in eagerness to see her. His nose was red on the end from being sick, and his eyes were puffy, but he didn't seem to care. And judging from the way her face lit up when she saw him, she didn't mind either.

"Maya!" he said, smiling. "Get my note?"

She nodded shyly.

"Great. I gotta head to class, but I wanted to see you first." He started to lean in close to her, then jerked back, as if unable to decide what was appropriate. Finally, he just grabbed her hand and pumped it up and down enthusiastically, then took off down the hallway.

Maya busted up giggling. "Did he just shake my hand?"

"Hey, he was just nervous," I said, laughing. "I can understand that. You know, you *are* a super hottie today."

"You sure are," Josh said to Maya from behind her. He slipped right in between her and me, turning his back to me.

"Oh, hi Josh!" she said, then started down the hall with him, not even noticing me anymore. "I didn't see you there. How was chem lab?"

I slowed my speed, letting them walk off together. I'd already had enough fun being the third wheel and didn't relish jumping back into it anytime soon. I shifted my notebook and *Jane Eyre* to my other arm and headed toward my locker, keeping my eyes peeled in case I was lucky enough to catch a glimpse of Derek.

Beside the stairs, I noticed Matthew and Britney, my first cupid match, standing close together. Matthew stroked the side of her face with his palm, then planted a small kiss on her forehead.

Britney sighed, a satisfied smile on her face, and took off upstairs. A week and a half in, and the magic clearly was still going strong.

Two of Matthew's buddies snickered as they approached him. "Dude, I can't believe how whipped you are," one said, shaking his head.

"Yeah, yeah," Matthew replied, rolling his eyes. "Laugh now, but we'll see how you feel when you find someone."

The three of them headed down the hall.

A warm feeling of joy swept over me. Look at what a great job I had done with the two of them! Matthew was enamored, totally swept off his feet for Britney. And she was obviously just as wrapped up in him.

Man, it hurt to be this talented at matchmaking. I wanted to proclaim right there in the hallway, *See those two people? I helped them find love!* Of course, I couldn't, so I settled for a tiny squeal under my breath.

"You okay, Felicity?" a guy's voice asked from right behind me.

I spun around, nearly smacking headfirst into Bobby Loward. I bit back a sigh.

Bobby Blowhard, as everyone in school called him, was a weird guy, to say the least. And he was about five foot two on a good day, which put him at eye level with me.

He also had a severe case of short-man's syndrome. You know, where little guys act big and tough in order to make up for their lack of height. So, he wore his brown hair in a "tough," spiky style and pumped iron a lot.

Well, I assumed he did, anyway. He was always talking about how much he lifted. I couldn't count the number of times he rubbed his arm muscles in front of me, yapping on about all the reps he'd finished that day.

Like I, or any other girl in school, cared. Poor, delusional Bobby.

"Hi, Bobby," I muttered, trying not to look irritated. Or make eye contact with his black mesh shirt.

Ew. I mean, come on—I could see his little man nipples poking through the holes. How was that even allowed? I thought clothing you could see through was against school rules. He should get sent home.

"I totally blew out my quads yesterday," he bragged, moving even closer to me. "Did three hundred pounds on the leg press." He looked down at his thighs and flexed the muscles. "Gotta keep in top shape, though, if I'm gonna top my own wrestling record next year."

"Gee," I said, wracking my brain for something nice to say. "Well, good luck." Rocking up on my toes, I looked over his shoulder, trying to plan my escape. Being trapped in a conversation with Bobby Blowhard was as bad as doing your own dental surgery, sans anesthesia.

And I should know—I mean, about dealing with Bobby, not about the dental surgery. He and I shared two classes together, health and math, so I always had to hear him spout off about something.

For some reason, Bobby had a crush on me. Maybe because I tried to be nice to him, even though he was odd. I kind of felt bad for him, since most people couldn't stand him. But it just figured. The one guy in the entire school who actually liked me had to be Bobby Blowhard.

He leaned in closer, now flexing his pecs at me too. If I didn't know better, I'd think he was having a seizure, with all the body twitches going on right now. "So, Felicity, what are you doing this weekend?"

Oh, God. Was he going to ask me out on a date?

I backed away, trying not to flinch at his creepy smile and dancing man-boobs, then glanced at my watch. "Oh, geez. Would you look at that? I gotta run. My American history class will probably start any minute, and I'm sure everyone will be inside soon. See ya later!"

I smiled and waved, turning to walk at breakneck speed. Time to get the hell out of Dodge before being guilted into something I didn't want to do.

Chapter 8

I ducked into American history, relieved by my narrow escape. No way did I want to get stuck going on a date with Bobby. And to ask me in front of everyone in the hallway, where people could overhear him? What if Derek saw Bobby leaning that close to me and assumed we were a couple? He'd probably never consider touching me after that. Okay, not that he was considering it, anyway, but still.

I flipped open my notebook and history book. We were wrapping up a lengthy discussion on the Great Depression—my English and history teachers liked to coordinate their lessons sometimes. Stupid me, I'd forgotten to read the required chapters last night because of going on Maya's date, but luckily, Mr. Shrupe went over everything in the book, so I didn't stress too hard.

Mr. Shrupe stood in front of the class, wearing his requisite white dress shirt, brown plaid sweater vest, and brown pants. His brown hair was parted perfectly on the side and slicked down across the top of his head. I swear, it would kill the guy to throw a little zazz in his wardrobe. He must get color-coordination tips from Maya or something.

"Today, we're going to wrap up our discussion about the—" Mr. Shrupe paused, waiting for the answer. No one replied. "Great Depression," he filled in, his voice droning. "That's right."

A couple of students groaned in misery, but he didn't seem to hear. Mr. Shrupe was certainly focused on history, if not fashion.

He wrote a few key words about the Great Depression on the board:

stock market crash/Black Tuesday
dust bowl
the New Deal

"And the Great Depression mainly occurred during the—" He paused. No answer again. *Duh.* "The nineteen thirties. That's right."

To keep from stabbing myself in the eye with my pencil from the sheer torture of enduring this lecture, I grabbed my PDA and nestled it in my lap. It was time to distract myself with something useful—making more successful love matches. If I could find more well-suited couples like Britney and Matthew, I'd be floating in bonus money in no time at all.

As visions of all the new shoes and super-hottie clothes I'd buy danced through my mind, I flipped through my database to find DeShawn's profile, which apparently, I'd filled out on a mega-cranky day:

Name: DeShawn Wallace

Age: 17

Interests: Himself

Style: Jock (and smart-ass)

Okay, I needed a bit more to go on than that. I forced myself to think of anything positive about DeShawn. It took me several minutes, but something did finally pop up: He likes to crack jokes. I added "sports" and "strong sense of humor" to his profile.

Who could I pair DeShawn up with? I flipped through the

profiles of all the girls in my database. One, oddly enough, jumped out at me:

Name: Marisa Dwight

Age: 16

Interests: Poetry, romantic encounters, journaling. Loves Shakespeare, as well.

Style: Smart, but popular

Marisa's a smart chick who is leagues above everyone else. She has perfect skin, can rock a poetry slam like nobody's business, and has legs longer than my entire body. She can also spout Shakespeare sonnets at whim and is probably going to one of those Ivy League schools when she graduates next year.

Could the two of them make it work as a couple? Well, Shakespeare was a great comedy writer, right? Plus, he wrote all those sword-fighting scenes . . . couldn't that count as a sports interest?

And, most importantly, dating Marisa would give DeShawn something positive to aspire for. He'd be inspired to learn the finer arts of wooing, an activity that could only do him some good.

A smart, pulled-together girl like Marisa was exactly what he needed.

A small part of me whispered that I was stretching this one big-time. But then again, hadn't I stretched it with Britney and Matthew? Look at how well that worked . . . lightning could strike twice, couldn't it? Or three times, if you counted Maya's matches. I told my doubting inner voice to shut it.

I composed my love match e-mail to the two of them and hit send, then put away my PDA and tried my best to focus on the rest of Mr. Shrupe's lecture.

I couldn't wait to see what happened when Marisa and DeShawn fell in love.

"Is spring really just around the corner?" I mused aloud to my mom that evening, running my finger along Target's shelf of fake green plants. "Because it sure doesn't feel like it."

Mom nodded, studying a ceramic green vase closely. "It'll be warm before you know it," she replied, flipping up the bottom of the vase to check out the price.

We'd decided to go browsing at Target, just to get out of the house for a while. Or at least, that's what I'd told her when I'd suggested the idea. In reality, I was scouting around for the perfect twenty-fifth-anniversary present for my folks, as the big day was less than a couple of weeks away.

Typically, my folks keep their celebrations low-key, so Rob and I don't normally get gifts except for the big milestones. But whenever those anniversaries have come around, I've procrastinated on getting them a present, waffling on what would be the perfect way to congratulate their lasting love. And every idea I've come up with has always been way too cliché or expensive.

So, my wishy-washiness inevitably meant me running out to the store the night before and getting them a card and some kitschy gift. For their twentieth anniversary, it was a Scooby-Doo head you could grow moss on, and a pair of soup mugs (I know—über lame, but in my defense, my parents love soup).

And this time was gearing up to be no different. Everything I'd looked at was either the wrong color, cost an arm and a leg, or was something they already had. Shopping for a couple is hard, especially my parents.

We made our way over to the clothing department. It seemed I wasn't going to have any luck tonight spotting them a good gift.

Well, I'd just borrow my mom's car in the next few days and hit another store without her.

Having come up with this tentative plan of action, I headed toward the aisles of bathing suits, ready to check out stuff for me. Sometimes, if I hit Mom on a good day, she'd splurge and buy me clothes.

"I can't believe they already have bathing suits out on the rack," I said.

Mom *mm-hm*'ed me noncommittally. Tough to tell whether she was feeling generous tonight or not.

I flipped through the bright, multicolored swimsuits and bikinis. Maybe there was something hiding on the rack that would make me look both super stacked and super skinny. Not likely, given the lovely pear shape of my body, but hey—a girl could hope.

Also, I was desperate for warmer temperatures to come, so maybe buying a bathing suit would remind the weather gods to send a little bit of sunshine our way.

My mom wrinkled her nose in disdain as she took in the teeny-tiny swimsuits in the juniors' section. With the tips of her fingers, she picked one up, her eyebrows shooting clean up into her hairline.

"This one's nothing more than hot-pink dental floss," she gasped, shaking her head. "Felicity, I don't want you wearing these. Can't you get a nice one-piece that will fully cover your buttocks?"

"Mom," I groaned, wishing she'd keep her voice a little quieter. She was such a prude. Besides, nobody says "buttocks" other than our health class teacher.

"I'm not going to wear one that shows everything, okay?" I said, trying hard to keep the whine out of my voice. "I just want to look nice."

Mom walked over to a rack in the women's section, which was right beside the juniors', thoughtfully studying the wares. "Look, this one has a lovely cover-up wrap," she cooed, holding up a bathing suit that had to have come straight from the 1920s, complete with thickly knit fabric in horizontal blue and white stripes. "And this one has shorts!"

Great. Just what I needed—to look like a grandmother. I mean, no offense to my grandma, who's the coolest woman I know, but I'm not in my seventies, for crap's sake.

I grabbed an adorable red two-piece suit, then took off down the aisle. "Going to the dressing room, okay?" I threw out over my shoulder.

After pulling shut the changing room door, I stripped to my bra and panties as fast as I could, then slipped on the two-piece. Surprisingly, the boy-cut bottoms fit nicely. I checked it out in the mirror, trying to ignore the panty lumps under the fabric.

The halter top, however, was too big. I'd inadvertently grabbed a size C-cup. Damn my non–C-cup chest! Maybe Mom could bring me the next smaller size.

I threw my coat on over the bikini, quickly slipped into my tennis shoes, then tiptoed to the front entrance of the changing room.

"Mom," I whispered. No answer. I tried again, a bit louder. "Mom, you there?"

"What do you need, Felicity?" she asked from about thirty feet away. She was still looking at old-lady bathing suits, probably trying to find me one that came with a turtleneck.

"Can you get me a different top?" I asked. "It's the dark red bikini halter top on the front rack."

"Sure thing," she bellowed back. "What size?"

I groaned and glanced at the lady working the changing room, who stared back at me with a slightly hostile look on her face. She looked like she trusted me about as far as she could throw me. And she certainly wasn't offering to help.

"Thirty-four B," I said as quietly as possible.

I heard Mom snort. "Did you say thirty-four D? With those little apples? Let's not delude ourselves, honey. You're more like an A-cup."

The dressing room attendant smothered a chortle behind her hand.

My entire face flamed with heat. "Mom!" Could this get any worse? "I said B-cup!"

"Felicity? Is that you?" a devastatingly familiar voice said from the guys' department, which was located just to the right of the women's changing rooms.

As if in a horror flick, I turned slowly, the blood draining from my face. Yup, my worst nightmare, come to life. Derek, the boy of my dreams, the hottie who had captured my heart, the guy I had been trying desperately to make notice me all year long, had just heard me announce my chest size. And probably my mom's "little apples" comment too.

I waited for my life to end. No such luck.

Derek placed the black pinstriped dress shirt he'd been looking at back on the rack, then came over to me in a slow, sexy saunter. At that moment I became acutely aware of the unfortunate fact that I was dressed in nothing more than a loose-fitting halter top, a lumpy bikini bottom, my coat, and a pair of sneakers. *Très* sexy.

I smoothed a hand over my hair and tried to look relaxed, like I always hung out in bikinis and winter coats and knew I looked fabulous. "Oh, Derek. I didn't know you shopped."

He chuckled, raising an eyebrow at my words.

"I mean, I didn't know you shopped here. At Target, I mean," I stumbled, wanting to kick myself for sounding so stupid. Time to cram my tennis shoe in my mouth. "Do you come here often?"

Someone, stop me from talking!

"Honey, I found the perfect—" My mom stopped dead in her tracks, staring at Derek in blatantly open interest.

Oh no, here it comes. The Target Inquisition.

"Hello," my mom said to Derek in a deceptively gentle voice. With one hand aimed at me, she thrust into my arms the smaller red halter bikini top, plus a wretched one-piece covered in hot-pink paisley, then stuck out the other hand toward him.

"Are you one of Felicity's . . . friends?" she asked, her beady eyes taking in my embarrassed look. "I'm her mom. Nice to meet you."

Derek, bless his heart, just smiled wider and shook her hand heartily. "I'm Derek. I go to Greenville High too."

Okay, time to end this introduction before I was forced to pray for a fiery meteor to hit the store.

"Well," I interjected, "I'm trying on bathing suits, so I'd better get back to it. It was nice seeing you, Derek." I pasted on my fake huge, bright smile.

He smirked, then nodded. "See ya, Felicity." With that, he strolled off toward the electronics department.

I tried not to watch him walk away, knowing my mom would totally harass me for staring at his cute butt. Instead, I turned back into the dressing room, stripped off the bikini, and threw on my regular clothes, too depressed to even try on the smaller top.

How was I ever going to face him again after the way that went down? And why do these things always happen to me? I'd spent so long practically worshipping at Derek's feet, wishing I could snag his attention.

Well, this was *not* the way I'd wanted to accomplish that goal.

Chapter 9

"It was so mortifying. I'll be scarred for life. My future therapist should thank my mom for all the shrink bills I'm going to run up," I whined, studying my freshly made-up reflection in the small handheld mirror.

Maya, Andy, and I were sprawled out in our jammies at Maya's house for our TGIF sleepover. Her parents had gone to bed a couple of hours ago, and I'd just finished sharing the Target bikini debacle with the two of them.

"And the worst part is," I continued, digging into the Clinique gift bag of makeup samples I'd received for buying another much-needed bottle of facial lotion, "Derek heard my mom say I was probably only an A-cup. There's, like, no way to do damage control on that."

"That's worse than him seeing you dressed in a lumpy bikini

bottom and falling-off top?" Andy asked, so not helpfully.

I tried to smile. "Don't forget the winter coat too. That really pulled the whole look together."

At least that was the only disastrous thing that had happened since then. The last couple of days I'd kept myself busy with homework and tried to avoid Derek at all costs. Which was virtually impossible, given that we shared a class together. The best I could do in art class, then, was keep my eyes firmly fixed on the project at hand, a linoleum cutting on the subject of our choice that we would use to make prints.

I'd found a picture of a woman's face in a magazine to do for mine. She was reclining, her face turned in a three-quarter profile toward the viewer. It was challenging, required my full attention, and thus, was a godsend.

However, I'd sensed Derek's eyes on me every once in a while. Or maybe that wasn't really happening and I'd been just hallucinating it, because I'd refused to look up and risk eye contact. But my Spidey senses had been tingling.

"Poor thing. Did you at least have shaved legs?" Maya asked, scrutinizing my face. She grabbed the eye shadow container and took the applicator in her hand, sliding a bit more of the dark brown shadow in the crease of my eyelids.

I kept my eyes closed and stayed motionless, not wanting to lose an eyeball. "Yes, thank heaven for that," I mumbled.

"Well, that sucks. Your mom kills me sometimes. And I thought mine was bad." Andy took a swig of strawberry wine cooler, then passed the bottle into my hand. She had smuggled it from her parents' house, and she and Maya were taking turns sipping from the bottle.

Honestly, I was surprised Maya was drinking any, since she wasn't a party girl, but I guess she felt comfortable enough around us to give it a whirl.

"I don't want any, thanks," I said, setting the bottle on Maya's nightstand. "The last thing I need is to get ripped." I hadn't been to a lot of parties, but I'd been to enough of them to know how stupid people looked when trashed.

"Ripped from a wine cooler?" Andy snorted. "Right. Honey, we're sharing the bottle. It won't be enough to give any of us more than a buzz, at most."

She had a good point. I took a tiny drink, the sweet liquid bubbling instantly in my mouth. "Hey, that's pretty good," I said, handing it back to her. "So, Maya, how was your first week as a love goddess?"

"Hardy har," she said, rolling her eyes. "I'm hardly a goddess."

"Don't underestimate yourself." Andy took a sip of the wine and passed the bottle to Maya. "You've managed to attract *and* sustain the attention of three hotties. That's no small feat."

She shrugged, taking a sip. "Yeah, I guess it's not too bad. It's just a lot to juggle. Ben's taking me out tomorrow afternoon for lunch and a movie, Quentin's meeting me for ice cream that evening, and Josh wanted to have Sunday brunch." She put the bottle down and sighed. "How am I going to choose between them? I feel bad for putting it off, but I like all of them."

"I'm sure you'll figure out something," I said. "But in the meantime, we can go over your schedule one more time to make sure we covered all the bases, if you're still feeling nervous about it."

On Thursday, I'd helped Maya come up with a plan to keep her love life balanced. It was an intricate chart, woven with incredible skill and finesse, breaking down which day and after which period she'd walk with each guy, with whom she'd share lunch, and on which nights they would date. I had to say, I'd outdone myself. Even Andy gave me kudos on the plan.

And the best part was, since Maya was dividing her attention equally, we could keep the rumor mill at bay, because there was no one guy she could be attached to. All in all, a success, if I did say so myself.

And not just with Maya's love match. Britney and Matthew were still going strong too. I'd overheard them in the halls talking about some indie band they'd seen on Wednesday night, holding hands and smiling into each other's faces. They still looked crazy about each other.

Even DeShawn's and Marisa's match was working out great so far. I'd noticed the two of them spending a lot of time in each other's company. She walked him to class every day, and they sat together at lunch, heads tucked closely together as they talked. Even though her friends weren't thrilled about the pairing, given the glares they gave DeShawn behind his back, Marisa didn't let it deter her from being with DeShawn.

And, much to my amusement, DeShawn now spent our English classes poring over *Jane Eyre* and listening to what the other students—females, especially—had to say about the romantic aspects of the book. Was he taking mental notes? Even our English teacher noticed the difference in his attitude, commenting on how quiet and attentive he was lately. I think she suspected him of brewing something sinister in his mind, but I knew the truth.

As for me, I secretly reveled in having brought DeShawn and Marisa together, a love match against all odds. I was getting really good at this. No wonder Janet had hired me—maybe I had a natural flair for romance and love.

Even though I still hadn't read the cupid guidebook or followed the rules to the letter, everything seemed to be working out great. Following my natural instinct was clearly way better than going by the book. After all, this was love, not rocket science.

A weird sound outside Maya's window caught my attention. I paused and cocked my head. "Did you guys hear something?"

A few tinkling thuds hit the window right when I finished my words.

We all jumped, and I let out an involuntary squeak.

Maya leaped from the floor and dashed to her window, peeking between the slots of her blinds. "What was that? What if it's a burglar?"

"It's not a burglar," Andy said, rolling her eyes. "What are they gonna steal, your trumpet?"

Maya leaned closer to the window. "Oh my God," she whispered, her voice suddenly breathy and soft. "It's Josh. He's here! Do I look okay?" She grabbed the mirror from my hand to study her reflection, checking the makeup job I'd done for her.

"Josh?" Andy stood, her eyes wide in surprise. "What's he doing here?" She pulled up the blinds and threw open the window, letting in a swift, chilly draft of air.

I grabbed a blanket to ward off the cold and cover my French poodle pajama bottoms. I'd already been spotted in one mortifying outfit that week, and once was enough. "Hey, close that window. It's fricking freezing!"

Andy stuck her head out. "Josh, stop throwing rocks!" she hissed. "You're gonna wake up Maya's parents!"

Oh God, she was right. That would be extra bad, especially since we had a wine cooler up here. What if Maya's parents found it? What if they had us arrested for teen drunkenness and we were thrown in jail?

My mom would never let me out of the house again. I'd have to quit my job, and maybe even be homeschooled, locked away in my bedroom with no outside contact. I'd never get to see Andy or Maya or Derek again.

I grabbed the bottle and thrust it toward Andy. "Pour it out," I said, my voice shaking. "And hide the bottle. I don't want Maya's parents to bust us with it."

"Andy, is that you? Where's Maya?" Josh's voice carried up into Maya's second-floor room.

Maya peeked her head over Andy's shoulder, shivering slightly as another gust of cold air swept into the room. "Hi, Josh. I'm right here," she said, waggling her fingers at him in greeting. "What's going on?"

Andy slipped away from the window, then handed me back the bottle. "I'm not pouring it out. That's wasting good wine. Just chug it."

"It's a cheap wine cooler—I'd hardly call it 'good.' And I'm *not* chugging it. *You* chug it." My luck, I'd be the one person in the world to get alcohol poisoning and die from chugging part of a wine cooler. How lame would that be?

"Maya," I heard Josh say, "I couldn't sleep. All I could think about was you. So I snuck out to see you."

Andy took a big swig of the wine, then leaned back out the window. "Josh, that was so sweet!"

Maya shot her a look, and Andy backed off.

"Geez, I wasn't being a smart-ass. It really *is*," she mumbled, plopping down on Maya's bed.

I stood up and peeked over Maya's shoulder to see Josh staring up at the window, his neck craned up. He clutched a bouquet of a dozen roses in his hands.

"He brought you flowers too?" I said, surprised. "Wow, that *is* sweet."

No one had ever snuck out and given me flowers at midnight. Or at any time, really.

"Who else is up there with you?" Josh asked Maya. "Are you having a party?"

I stuck my hand out the window and waved at him, then quickly pulled it back in, rubbing warmth back into my frozen fingers. Damn, it was cold out there. How could he stand it? I guess the power of love was warming him from within. Gag.

I could understand the compulsion, though. I'd probably stand out all night in an arctic blizzard if it meant getting a chance to talk to Derek one-on-one. Okay, that was an exaggeration, but just a little one.

"That was Felicity," Maya said to Josh. "I'm having a sleepover."

"Felicity? Oh," he said, his voice uncomfortable. I knew he was remembering the bathroom incident at the movies.

Yeah, I didn't want to think about that, either. I stepped back to let them talk, sitting beside Andy on the bed.

"I brought you flowers," I heard him say. "Can you come to the door?"

"I can't. My parents' room is on the first floor." Maya's voice was filled with regret.

"Maybe he can fling them up here," I suggested.

"Good idea," she said to me, her face brightening. "Can you throw the flowers up to me?" she asked Josh.

"I'd really rather see you," he hedged. "But if you want them, here they are. Catch!"

We heard him huff as he tossed them up, and then a smashing thud as the bouquet hit the window, next to Maya's head, then fell back to the ground.

"Ow!" Maya gasped, clutching her brow. "I got scratched by a thorn! And I dropped the flowers!" She backed away from the window.

"Here, let me see it." I checked out Maya's war wound. It was a small scratch right in the middle of her forehead. A bead of blood bloomed at the spot of the injury.

I grabbed a tissue and wiped it away, pressing the tissue to the scratch. "It's . . . not that bad," I fudged.

"Are you sure?" Maya's face was pale and drawn. "Wait, what if this is an omen? A sign that I shouldn't be with Josh? What do I do now?"

"Maya, are you okay? Maya!" Josh's voice got louder, more anxious.

Andy leaned out the window. "Shh! She's fine. Hold on a sec." She turned to Maya. "Just go down and see him for a minute. Let him give you the flowers the right way instead of making him throw them at your face."

"But, my parents—" Maya protested.

"Just be quiet about it, and don't stay down there forever. You'll be fine," Andy said. She pushed Maya toward the door, then leaned out the window. "She's coming down."

Andy and I sat on the bed while Maya snuck downstairs. Andy shook her head. "That girl's a mess. I hope when she picks one of them, she'll settle down into being a bit more normal."

"So, who do you think she should pick?" I asked.

In all honesty, I'd had no indication from Maya on which guy she liked best so far. All three of them were different, and all appealed to various aspects of her. With Josh, Maya was able to discuss and enjoy weird and off-the-wall movies or music, because he was into that too. Quentin brought out her romantic nature through discussions of literature, art, and poetry. And she loved that Ben reached outside his comfort zone to show her his feelings.

But she showed the same level of affection to each of them and talked about them with equal excitement and uncertainty, so there were no external indicators to show me which one she preferred.

I could see, though, that the attention from the guys was causing a slow, but definite change over Maya. I'd never seen her fuss over makeup before. She smiled more in public now, walked down the halls with more confidence and bounce. She'd never seemed so comfortable in her skin before. But then again, she'd never had a guy try to bring her flowers at midnight before either.

"I don't know." Andy shrugged. "It's hard to tell. She's her own person, and even if I like one guy better than the others, Maya won't be influenced by anyone else when making a decision as big as that."

I nodded. "Yeah, I guess you're right." That was, after all, why I'd wanted to let her choose for herself in the first place.

After another minute, we heard the bedroom door creak open. I lunged to cover the wine cooler with a blanket, but it was only Maya, her entire face aglow. She held the bouquet in her arms, pressing the blossoms to her face.

"Aren't they beautiful?" she said, her eyes shiny. "I've never had anyone bring me flowers before."

At that moment, I realized what a vast difference being in love (well, at least, one-third in love) did for Maya. She looked flushed, a bit erratic, but very, very pretty. Even with the little bloody dot on the middle of her forehead, she looked great.

But it was not just loving someone. It was *being* loved by that person—or, those people—in return. Having someone reciprocate those feelings made everything feel right.

"They really are gorgeous," I said, rising to go hug her and smell them for myself. After all, those roses were probably the closest I was going to get to that all-encompassing kind of love.

Chapter 10

"Bye, Rob," my mom said, holding the front door open with her hip as my brother headed out the house after dinner that Sunday. She squeezed him close. "Don't be a stranger," she added, her tone slightly chastising. "We never hear from you during the week. You *can* call us, you know."

"Yeah, yeah," he mumbled. He gave my mom a peck on the cheek and clenched the large bag of leftovers in his hand. Mom always sent him home with food, which was a good thing, because Rob couldn't cook to save his life. When he wasn't eating Mom's food, he probably had takeout every night at his apartment. Which was also a good thing, because it kept him from burning down his place.

Rob had come alone to Sunday dinner this week, no date in tow.

I figured the blond fluffbag had already dumped him. None of us had even bothered to ask where she was, that's how cynical we were about his love life.

"Thanks again for dinner," he said. "See ya guys next week." He took off down the front steps.

Mom closed the door behind him, then darted into the kitchen, probably to microwave a bag of butter-laden popcorn, as she did every Sunday night.

"It's almost eight, Becky," my dad called to her from the living room. He sank onto his plush dark brown recliner, clicking the TV on with the huge cable remote, then pushed up the footrest using the handle on the side of the chair.

"What's on tonight?" Mom asked, returning from the kitchen bearing a bowl of popcorn and settling onto the couch.

"Not sure. Let me look." He turned on the cable guide, scrolling through the list of shows.

It was my parents' tradition after Sunday dinner to watch a movie together. They'd been doing this religiously every weekend for as long as I could remember. When I didn't have homework to do, I'd join them if I was interested in whatever movie they were watching.

Mom often picked the old romantics on the American Movie

Classics channel, laughing at the sharp banter between the leading couples. I loved watching the antics of those early Hollywood actors too.

My dad, however, tended to be drawn to epic movies like *The Godfather* trilogy. Mom hadn't loved these, but I'd gotten totally caught up in the drama of that infamous Mafia family, the Corleones. Watching those people spend money hand over fist made me wish I had a more exciting home life, but I guess being surrounded by danger and destruction isn't really such a good thing.

As thrilling as it would be to be the daughter of a mob boss, we were all better off with my dad working in the mortgage department of the bank. A bit on the boring side, yes, but less prone to death.

"Hey, Dad," I said, snagging a handful of popcorn from Mom's bowl, "what are you two doing for your anniversary?" Maybe if I pried into their plans, I could get an idea for the ultimate present.

He shrugged, continuing to flip through the channel guide. "Probably the same thing we do every year. You know I love El Rincon's enchilada platter."

Mom eyed the TV. "Maybe we can check out that Japanese

restaurant in North Olmsted, instead. Oh, flip back to the Turner Classics," she said, waving her finger at the screen.

Dad blanched. "I hate sushi."

"How do you know if you hate it?" Mom must have realized how edgy her voice sounded, because she gave a small smile. "You've never tried it. You might like it." She put the popcorn bowl down on the coffee table.

Dad gave a grunt in reply and kept his eye on the screen.

Yikes. This was no help at all. If they kept bickering like that, their milestone anniversary wasn't going to be much to cele-brate.

I chewed on my handful of popcorn. Come to think of it, when was the last time I saw the two of them dress up and have a special night out on the town? They basically only ever went out together one night a year on their anniversary, and even then, they could barely be bothered to make the night romantic.

I racked my brain to remember their past dates. One particular anniversary came to mind—when Rob and I were little, our sitter cancelled at the last minute. So, Mom and Dad took us to Chuck E. Cheese for their anniversary because Rob pitched a fit and refused to eat anywhere else.

That night got even worse when Rob pulled off the Whack-a-Mole hammer and thwacked me over the head with it, causing a flurry of screams and tears. The jerk. He was built for a life of whomping on others. He'd make a fantastic prison warden, for sure.

Now that I was older, I could appreciate how bad that must have been for my parents. Spending your anniversary with two whiny kids? Sucksville.

Year after year of their anniversaries flipped through my mind, a never-ending series of nonspectacular non-events. Dinner at a Chinese buffet. Dinner at El Rincon. Dinner at home because I had the flu. Dinner at a Chinese buffet. Dinner and a movie that my dad hated and griped about for weeks after. And my all-time favorite . . . dinner at Burger Butler, when Rob did a fake burp and ended up puking all over Mom.

A sudden alarm darted through my veins, and I stared at the two of them, taking in their attitudes about their own anniversary—especially my dad's utter unwillingness to try something new. Was the magic gone for them?

Wait, had the magic ever been there in the first place?

I thought about the love matches I'd made at school, the rush of feelings sparking almost visual fires between my couples. Even

Maya, who was only one-third in love, had more chemistry with the three guys than my folks had together.

Had my parents ever been like that? Looking at them now, one wouldn't think so.

Wait. A flutter of excitement tickled inside my chest. I hopped out of my seat and flew upstairs, turning my PC on as I ran an utterly inspired idea through my mind.

I logged into my blog, making it a diary entry so that I was the only one who could see it, then started to type.

I think I figured out what to do for my parents. Finally! Maybe the best gift I can give them for this milestone anniversary isn't one bought in a store—though I'll still get them a card, of course.

Maybe in this case, the gift of love is much more needed. And I'm the perfect person to help with that.

I could send my mom and dad the love e-mails, and not even count it as a love match—it could be a side project. As a cupid, I've learned to appreciate romance in general, especially lasting matches. Why should my folks be any different?

I continued with my diary entry.

The big question is, will it work between two people already in a relationship?

Well, there was only one way for me to find out.

"So, why is Jane Eyre drawn to a man like Mr. Rochester?" Mrs. Kendel asked our English class bright and early on Monday morning. She paced up and down the aisles, her long skirt swishing around her thick legs. "Rochester is gruff, rude, sometimes downright hostile . . . and yet, she falls in love with him." She stopped and scratched her chin, her head tilted. "What does this say about Jane and, even more importantly, what does it say about society and women's expectations during Jane's time period?"

Silence. Either no one knew the answer, no one cared, or no one was awake enough yet to articulate any halfway decent thoughts.

I raised my hand.

"Miss Walker," Mrs. Kendel said to me with a small smile, almost looking grateful that I was going to take a stab at it. "Please, go ahead."

"Well," I started in a hesitant voice, "even though Mr. Rochester is far from perfect, Jane feels he's perfect for her." Out of the corner of my eye, I noticed DeShawn staring at me with an odd look on his face.

At that moment, a profound thought hit me—DeShawn was kind of like Mr. Rochester. Gruff, rude, and sometimes downright hostile, but there had to be goodness deep inside. Maybe Marisa would be his Jane. How romantic!

"Mr. Rochester's made mistakes. He did things that embarrassed people unnecessarily," I continued, thinking about DeShawn and the unfortunate pantsing incident, "but Jane can see he's a good man on the inside. He just needs to work harder on showing her he deserves her love, long-term."

Yeah, I was laying it on a bit thick, but I hoped my words were getting through to DeShawn. After all, I didn't think Mrs. Kendel would appreciate me outright saying that Mr. Rochester-slash-DeShawn needed to stop being an ass permanently if he was gonna keep the love going. Though Deshawn and Marisa's relationship was solid right now, there was no guarantee it would continue that way—especially if he converted back to his old antics after the spell wore off.

Just this morning, when Marisa and DeShawn had split ways to head to their separate classes, I'd overheard Marisa's friends giving her flack again for being with DeShawn, saying she could do better than him. To be honest, I think most of us—and maybe even Marisa herself—knew this was a precarious pairing. Because of that, I felt obligated to do my part and steer DeShawn in the right direction. Hopefully, he'd pick up the hints I was throwing his way.

DeShawn looked away from me, staring at his notebook. He rubbed a hand over his jaw, deep in thought.

"Thanks, Miss Walker," Mrs. Kendel said. "Those are valid points. I think you'll see this novel also reflects how the Victorian society viewed relationships. Rochester has the upper hand, both as a male and as Jane's employer. As we read on, we'll see what happens to change the dynamic of this relationship and how the power shifts from Rochester to Jane."

The rest of the class period went by fast. When the bell rang, Maya gave me a quick hug, then darted out the door to meet Ben, who was scheduled to walk her to second period.

"Hey," DeShawn grunted at me after the guys around him left the classroom. "You're a girl, right?"

Gee, was it that obvious? Swallowing my instinctively snarky reply, I simply nodded.

"If a guy wanted to impress a girl—a smart girl—and really

show how he . . . cared, what could he do?" DeShawn's hands fiddled with the hem of his shirt.

Oh. My. God. DeShawn was asking me for love advice! It had worked—I'd gotten through to him!

I grabbed my books in the calmest manner possible, cradling them in the crook of my arm. I needed to weigh my words carefully—one wrong phrase could screw everything up.

"Well," I said, "for a girl like that, a guy should appeal to her heart *and* her brain. She'd appreciate someone reaching her intellectually."

"But how? Should I buy her something, like a book?"

We headed out the door, him walking beside me. I never thought this day would come, the day DeShawn and I would walk side by side down the hallway like friends. It was like a UN peace treaty had been signed between two warring countries, and it was all because of the cupid spell.

Amazing, the power of love.

"Well, you can buy her presents," I answered, "but smart girls really appreciate gifts that come from the heart." I paused, trying to think of the best answer. What would be the perfect gift for her? "Mari—um, smart girls often love handwritten poetry. I mean, you saw how well it worked for Quentin on Maya."

He cringed. "I can't write that junk."

I nodded, feeling unexpected sympathy with him. "Honestly, I can't either," I confided. "But if you care about someone, isn't it worth trying something difficult to prove your feelings?"

"I guess so." By the tone of his voice, he didn't sound too convinced.

"Hey, what about haiku?" *Oh, Felicity, a brilliant idea!* I congratulated myself. My words spilled out in an excited rush. "Those are short and easy to write, but very poetic. They're only three lines long, but they pack a lot of punch." Boy, my tenth-grade English teacher would be proud to hear me now.

DeShawn gave me a seemingly indifferent shrug, but I could tell by the look on his face that he was considering my suggestion. "Yeah, I remember. So, I should just write about flowers and sunsets and other girly stuff, right?"

I smothered a giggle with an exaggerated cough, pressing my clenched fist to my mouth. This was not the time to laugh. "Yup, that's right." I stopped in front of my American history class. "Well, this is my room. Good luck on the poem!"

"Later." DeShawn walked off.

I stared at his back for a moment before heading into class. That. Was totally. Surreal.

Chapter 11

"Felicity!" Maya called to me from outside her locker, waving frantically. When I got there, she leaned in and whispered, though not very quietly, "Wait till you hear this—Quentin wants to take my picture!"

"He does? What for, HottieTeenHoochies.com?" I teased her.

"Shut *up*." She slugged me in the upper arm, ignoring my cries of protest. "No, Quentin wants to feature me in the 'movers and shakers' part of the yearbook. He thinks the school should learn more about me and my accomplishments."

"Oh, that's so cool!" I said. "He takes really good pictures."

Maya paused, biting her lower lip, and her face fell a little. "Hm. Now that I'm thinking about it, maybe that's not the best idea. After all, I'm not like the divas around here who can wear sweat pants and no makeup and still look hot."

"Hey, no talking like that," I said, frowning. "Andy and I think you rock. Quentin thinks you're awesome. So do Ben and Josh. Just remember that." I could tell by how strongly they felt about her that their love would probably last past the spell, whichever one she finally chose, so I was confident in pointing this out.

Maya scrolled the lock on her locker door, shrugging a little. "I know you're right. I'm just panicking about this. I need a clear sign of which guy is the right one for me."

"Maybe you can get your palm read," I joked. "And you can also learn what college you'll go to and how many kids you're gonna have."

"That's actually not a bad idea." Maya flicked off the lock and tugged the door open, then sucked in a quick, startled breath. A flock of small, brightly colored helium balloons flew out of the tight locker space and up to the ceiling. It looked like a circus clown car being evacuated, there were so many balloons fleeing the locker.

"Oh my God!" she gasped, her eyes wide.

"Look! Balloons!" several people in the hallway said as they snatched at the thin white ribbons. Most of them handed the balloons back to Maya, though few jerky guys held on to theirs—probably to pop them behind whatever unsuspecting girls they could find. Idiots.

One cute guy handed Maya a couple of balloons back. "Here ya go," he said, a deep dimple in his right cheek as he shot her a smile.

"Oh, thanks!" she said to him, a bright blush staining her cheeks. "What a crazy surprise!"

Interesting development. Now *other* guys are flirting with Maya too? Must be something to this budding self-confidence of hers.

"Soooo," I drawled after the cute guy walked off, shifting my attention back to the bundle of balloons Maya held in her shaky grasp. "Who did that? Is there a card or something?"

And how did he get into her locker? I thought to myself. That part was a bit creepy, though I knew the gesture was meant to be sweet.

Maya poked her head in the locker, looking around. "I don't see any—oh, wait." She withdrew, holding an envelope. She peeled it open, staring at the contents for a moment. Without a word, she handed me the card.

I peeked at the front, a picture of two purple cartoon rabbits cuddling on a puffy pink couch. The card's inside was just as cheese-laden:

I got an idea—

Let's be snuggle bunnies!

Oh, gag. Who got paid to write this kind of crap? I tried my best not to roll my eyes as I read the handwritten inscription:

I hope these balloons brighten up your ~~morn~~ day!

Love,

Ben

I looked up at Maya. "Wow," I finally said.

She nodded slowly, then dramatically sighed, pressing her free hand to her chest. "No kidding. Wasn't that the sweetest thing ever? Maybe this was my sign—maybe *Ben* is the one. There's something about his quiet, deep nature that really draws me in. And these surprises he leaves me shows me I'm on his mind."

"It was very thoughtful of him," I said, nodding. "But we gotta head to class, so you'd better put the balloons back in your locker."

"Oh, good point," she said, scrunching up her nose. "I can't take these to anatomy."

It took both of us pushing to get those damn balloons in there, though a couple wouldn't fit. We picked the three smallest to pop, tossing the deflated balloons into the garbage bin a few feet away. How the hell had Ben fit all these into her locker in the first place, especially with Maya's trumpet case hogging up a large portion of room? He must have spent some serious time and effort.

The bell rang. Uh-oh, time for art class.

"See ya," I said to Maya, waving good-bye as I took off down the hall.

I headed my way to art, both dreading and looking forward to it. It was almost a delicious sort of torture, seeing Derek's striking face, hearing his low chuckle when someone said something that amused him. And when he laughed, his bright eyes crinkled in the corners. He was magnetic, and I just couldn't seem to get enough of him . . . even in spite of the bathing suit incident.

Inside the classroom, I grabbed my linoleum cutting and tools from the art shelf and slipped into my seat. Derek came in shortly after, heading right to the art shelf, as well.

Staring intently at my carving, I picked up the V-shaped knife, drew in a deep breath, then started digging into the shell of the ear I was etching.

"Can I sit here?" Derek asked from out of the blue, startling the crap out of me.

My hand jerked slightly, cutting off a bit too much linoleum. Whoops, there went the tip of her ear. Van Gogh would be proud.

I glanced up, up, up into his glorious sparking eyes looking down at me, and gave him a crooked smile.

Hello—speak, idiot!

"Um, why do you want to sit by me?" I blurted. Oh, geez, that sounded dumb. And rude. Why did I grill him about it instead of simply saying yes? I was a glutton for punishment.

He nodded his head toward his usual spot. "My spot's taken." Sure enough, some other guy was perched in Derek's usual chair.

"Sure, go ahead." I tugged the chair out for him, the feet squeaking across the floor.

He sat in the seat beside me, putting his project and sketching pencils on the table. He was still finalizing his picture before beginning to trace and carve his linoleum square. His project was an apple orchard scene on a farm, trees sprawling across the countryside down to the horizon. A rickety barn rested in the back right corner. The picture was good—very good.

God, was there anything Derek couldn't do? Hell, he could

probably jump right into a pilot's seat and land a freaking airplane if he wanted to.

"That's amazing," I said, a little breathless. I slid my hand over my own linoleum cutting, trying to obscure it from his vision. It wasn't horrible, but it certainly didn't compare to his work.

He chuckled, picking up a pencil and adding more definition to the tree nearest the bottom of the picture. "It's not that great, but thanks. I need to do a little more work on the shading."

I nodded, then looked back at my work. We did our art in companionable silence for a long stretch of time, and I found myself glancing back at him again and again. "So, why did you pick an orchard scene?" I finally asked him.

"Well, this was what my grandpa's farm looked like. I used to go there as a kid all the time and run between the rows of trees."

"Really?"

He laughed. "No, not really. I just thought it sounded more interesting than the truth. Actually, I saw the picture in a magazine and just picked it to draw." Then, he looked at me, a small grin still lingering on his face. "I guess I just like apples."

Apples? What did he—

Clarity came to me in a whirl of mortifying light. Derek was teasing me about my mom's comment in Target on my "little apples."

Or, wait. Was he . . . flirting?

The last bell of the day rang, and I dawdled out of the art room, wanting to prolong my time with Derek as much as possible. It was crazy, this compulsion to be around him. To keep him talking to me. Not that I seemed to say anything remotely intelligent when I did get him into a conversation.

I pushed my art project back in its spot on the shelf, shooting Derek's retreating figure one last glance, then gathered up my belongings and made my way back to my locker. There had to be a way to make Derek notice me that would not make me look like a dumb-ass this time.

I bet I could ask Andy and Maya to help me come up with something that didn't relate at all to my cupid matchmaking techniques. Then, Janet couldn't complain, because I wouldn't have done anything against my contract.

I shrugged into my coat and grabbed my backpack, then made my way through the school doors. Andy had to run an errand for her mom, and Maya had a date right after school, so I was hoofing it alone. The grounds were nearly emptied, except for a few people lingering on the steps.

A heavy thud, followed by rustling around the corner of the school building, got my attention.

"Careful!" I heard a guy say. "Don't squash that piece of cardboard. It's in perfect shape. We can recycle that."

"Sorry, honey. I'm—trying my—best," a girl replied, sounding breathless.

Curious, I rounded the corner to find Matthew and Britney, my first matchmade couple, waist-deep in two of the school's garbage dumpsters.

I stopped mid-stride at the sight. Britney had dark smudges across her face, from God only knew what. Her nose was red-tipped from the cold air, and she had clumps of unidentifiable stuff in her hair.

From his garbage bin, Matthew flung a few more pieces of garbage out onto the parking lot. "I can't believe people threw this away," he muttered to Britney, shaking his head. "Look at this!" He waved a small glass bottle in one gloved hand. "Do you know how easy it is to recycle glass?"

"What are you guys doing?" I asked, trying to keep my repulsion at their garbage-digging activity out of my voice.

Britney stopped mid-dig and stood up. "Oh, hey," she said to me, smiling. "Matthew likes to go garbage diving once a week and pull out the recyclables. So he asked me to join him today after school."

Was this a date? As for me, I'd rather have dinner and a movie, but they looked happy and were being productive, so I guess that's what counted.

"Well, that's great," I finally said.

"Actually, it's scary how much recyclable stuff I find in here," Matthew said to me, his eyes boring into mine. "If we don't take care of our environment, no one will." He stopped and raised one eyebrow. "You *do* recycle, don't you, Felicity?"

"Oh, absolutely," I answered quickly, instantly feeling a twinge of guilt. Okay, that wasn't the absolute truth, because I knew for a fact I wasn't *this* active about it. But I did throw old paper in the paper recycling bin—didn't that count for something?

Besides, I didn't have to dig through garbage to help the environment. There were lots of ways to pitch in and reduce, reuse, recycle. I totally avoided aerosol cans, so I was saving the ozone in my own way.

"That's great. Wanna help us out?" Matthew asked. "We still have a couple of garbage bins to go through." He pointed over to the two furthest garbage dumpsters, their lids flung open to reveal a mysterious pile of grossness.

"Ah!" Britney suddenly cried out, clinging to the side of her dumpster. "I think I slipped on something in here. Anyway," she said to me, righting herself, "it's not so bad once you get past the smell."

Ewwww. Yeah, that was appealing. I'd heard the nose was quick to adapt to stinky scents, but I didn't see how one could adapt to the school trash smell.

I lifted up the sleeve of my jacket, glancing at my watch, while secretly trying to cover my gagging mouth. "Oh, I'd love to," I choked out, "but I gotta head home. You know how parents are when you're late."

Not that my folks were home this early, but there was no way I was going to dig through the school garbage dumpsters. I saw the kinds of things people threw away, and no way did I want to reek like that.

"Okay, later," Britney said.

"You two have fun," I replied, heading back around the corner. I heard more stuff being flung onto the ground and shook my head.

To each his own, right?

Chapter 12

When I got home, I keyed the front door of my house and pushed it open, shuffling through. I needed some peanut butter fudge ice cream therapy, stat. The confusion over Derek's ambiguous words in art class had run round and round in my head throughout the rest of the period, and then on the walk home from school. Even in spite of Britney and Matthew's gross garbage-digging date.

What was going on with Derek? Was he actually trying to flirt with me, or was I just reading what I wanted to hear into the conversation? Why were guys so hard to interpret, anyway?

Regardless of his intent, I was seething anew over my mom's snarky public commentary on my chest size. Boy, was she gonna hear about it when she got home.

I pulled off my boots and hung my coat up, slogging into the house with my backpack over my shoulder. Right after ice-cream therapy, I needed to call Andy and dissect every word of the discussion. Maybe she'd help me find clarity.

Andy was pretty good at what I liked to call "guyomancy"—where you picked apart everything a guy said to interpret his true meaning. I couldn't count the number of evenings we sat on the phone and practiced this mystical art as old as time. Of course, it was usually more about Andy's dates than mine, but whatever.

This time, we'd have some good Derek stuff to talk about before I went to my weekly meeting with Janet in a couple of hours.

I dumped my backpack on the couch and headed toward the kitchen. I happened to glance over at the stairs. A pair of Dad's black socks was draped carelessly on plateau of the lowest step. They must have fallen out of Mom's laundry basket. I snagged them, then walked up to toss them into their bedroom. Geez, and there were Mom's panty hose, the toes drooped over the top step.

Maybe it was time for her to get a new laundry basket, given how much stuff was falling out. The House Nazi would go ballistic if *I'd* left my socks on the stairs. Nice double standard, Mom.

I grabbed the pantyhose too, then turned the corner at the top of the stairs and froze. Two pairs of naked feet were stretched out on the ground, sticking out my parents' bedroom doorway.

What the . . . ?

I heard a low chuckle. The toes on the small pair of feet wiggled, then rubbed along the inner arches of the big pair of feet.

Understanding cracked me over the head like Rob's Whack-a-Mole mallet. Those were my parents' feet!

"Aaaah!" I screeched.

The feet froze in place, then scrambled inside the room.

"Felicity, is that you?" my mom asked, her voice slightly muffled.

Horrified, I dropped the panty hose and socks in the hallway and booked it down the steps, almost tripping over my own feet. I grabbed my purse, threw on my shoes and coat, and ran out the front door, escaping into the brisk air.

As I headed down the sidewalk to Andy's house, I scrubbed my hand over my face. Maybe a few years of therapy would scrub that horrific image out of my head. Likely not.

I could just imagine that conversation now:

"Sex is natural," the doctor would tell me, her soothing voice like a balm to my grossed-out feelings. "It's wonderful for two people to share."

"But . . . but . . . they were on the floor. What were they sharing, carpet burn? And, hello, they knew I was coming home after school." I'd grab a tissue and cry for a few minutes, dabbing the corners of my eyes.

"That's it, cry it out." She'd pat me on the back. "You're making fantastic progress. Another decade or two of therapy, and you'll finally be almost normal. Oh, and here's your bill for the month," she'd say, handing me the invoice. "Wanna just sign your car over to me this time?"

Yeah, maybe even therapy wouldn't reduce the trauma. I strolled up Andy's walkway, cramming my hands into my coat pockets. I'd talk to her about it.

I stood on her stoop and lifted a fist to pound on her door, then paused. Maybe dumping this on her wasn't the best idea, after all. Why would she want to hear about my parents' extracurricular activities? I wouldn't want to hear this kind of pervy info about her folks, especially given her mom's inclination toward the superfreaky side of life. No need for everyone to be scarred.

Besides, this had all come about because of me and my brilliant anniversary present idea. The only reason my parents were all makey-outey all of a sudden was because of the love e-mail I'd sent them.

I had no one to blame but myself for this catastrophe.

Before I could walk away from Andy's house, though, the front door opened, with Andy herself in the doorway.

"Hey," she said to me, smiling. "Whatcha doing here? That's freaky, because I was just getting ready to call you. Mom didn't need me to get her a new yoga mat, after all. Thank. God." She dramatically rolled her eyes, then studied my face, no doubt seeing the utter misery etched into it. "Hey, you okay?"

"Remember this moment, Andy." I glanced at my watch. "Monday, three twenty-five p.m. This is the day I found out firsthand how much my parents like to—" I couldn't even finish the sentence. A wave of sickness rolled through my stomach at the memory of their rubbing feet, their giggles.

God, someone kill me now!

"Oh, noooo," Andy said, her eyebrows shooting straight up into her hairline. "You didn't catch them . . . ?"

"Andy," her mom said from inside the house, her light voice lilting over to us. "Close that door, would you? It's getting drafty in here. And come help me with this new pose. I can't get my leg up far enough."

Andy held a finger up to her mouth, fake gagging. "Fine, Mom,

I'll be there in a sec!" she shouted over her shoulder.

"Gee, that sounds like fun," I teased.

In a low whisper, Andy said to me, "Right. At this point, I'd rather bust my parents doing it than help my mom stretch her leg over her head. Maybe it's time to act on our old plan to join the carnival?"

I smothered a laugh. When Andy and I were in fourth grade, we'd mapped out what we thought was the perfect plan to run away from home. Of course, since we were only nine, it involved asking our parents to make us enough sandwiches to last us until we found jobs at a traveling carnival.

In retrospect, it wasn't the best idea ever, but the concept still had merit, given the current icky situation.

"Sounds like you got parental issues of your own to deal with right now," I said, shaking my head in sympathy. "Wanna meet at Starbucks this evening after I get out of my work meeting? Around six?"

"Okay, I'll see you there." Andy gave me a quick hug, then headed back inside.

I turned around and headed home, knowing it was time to face the music. When I rounded the corner to my street, my mom and dad were leaning out the front door, clad in long, thick black bathrobes. They peered down both sides of the sidewalk.

When Mom saw me, she waved her arm. "Felicity!" she yelled, her brows pinched together in concern. "Are you—were you—"

I nodded, unable to fight back the shudder as I got a flashback of the naked rubbing feet. "I am, and I was, thank you very much."

I broached our front steps and stopped.

She grabbed my arm and tugged me in. "It's freezing. Come inside."

I grudgingly followed her into the living room and plopped on the couch. Dad closed the door, and then they both stood in front of me, staring down.

"It's okay, sweetie," Mom said to Dad, resting a hand on his arm, "I can take it from here."

He whispered something in her ear, rubbing his hand up and down her arm. She giggled, her cheeks burning bright red.

"You're such a cad!" she said with a laugh, pushing him out of the room.

My gag reflex threatened to give. "Mo-o-o-ommm," I groaned. "You're grossing me out." What the hell had I done? That e-mail was a huge mistake. I'd had no idea they'd go from being normally indifferent, asexual parents to acting like a pair of horny teenagers.

Mom sat on the couch beside me, a smile lighting her face. It was almost creepy, because I'd never seen her so . . . glowing. "Felicity, when a man and a woman love each other—"

I held up a hand. "Ew. Don't go there. We had this talk a long time ago, remember?" I'd actually known about the birds and the bees for ten years now.

That's right. I got the sex talk at age *seven*. I was just an innocent young lass then, not knowing that The Talk lay in wait for me.

I remember one day in second grade, I'd asked Dad the meaning of "jumping her bones," a term I'd overheard Rob say to one of his friends. Dad's face had instantly paled, and after sucking in a few deep breaths, he'd mumbled something under his breath before pushing me out of the room.

But the very next night, Mom had knocked on my bedroom door, instruction books in hand. For the next hour and a half, she'd proceeded to burn the worst possible images ever into my tender young retinas.

But I'd taken her lesson to heart. I was now too freaked about pregnancy and worried about getting an STD to even think about putting out.

In front of me, Mom sighed, her shoulders sagging in relief. "Oh, good," she said. "Anyway, your father and I are sorry you had to see that. We love you." She kissed me on the cheek, then traipsed upstairs, giggling again.

I sank back into the couch with a groan. Was this what I had to look forward to every day?

The next two weeks couldn't go by fast enough.

"Thanks for meeting me," I told Andy as we stood inside the doorway of Starbucks. "I needed to get out of the house for a while. My parents are driving me crazy, so I told them I was going to go study with you for a little while."

Actually, my parents were fine with me being out of the house, as it gave them more alone time.

Ick. *Not* going to think about that right now.

Andy hugged me, and her laptop bag bumped against my side. "No problem," she said. "I wanted a break from my house, too. Mom's driving me insane with this yoga crap." She paused. "You know, it's too bad Maya's out on a date. I'm sure she's having more fun than we are, though."

We hopped into the coffee line, right behind a couple of

businesswomen in matching dark blue pantsuits. They took about a billion years each to order a half-caff double whippy mocha java thingamajig.

Good grief. I kept it simple for the poor barista and got an iced mocha. Andy ordered her standard black coffee, no sugar or creamer.

Yuck. I don't know how she drank those. I'd be shaking like crazy from that much caffeine overload, not to mention be sick to my stomach. Plus, I like a bunch of sugar. But black coffee totally fit Andy's personality: straightforward with no messing around—what you see is what you get.

When our drinks had been prepared, we snagged a table near the back. Andy pulled her laptop out, plugging it into the outlet beside her.

"It sounded to me like you needed some cheering up," she said, a mischievous smile on her face as she flipped open the laptop, a present from her mom and dad for her birthday this year. "When you're down, I know there's one thing that always cheers you up."

"And what's that?"

"Our favorite activity—besides ripping on people at school, of course. Ripping on your brother." She booted the computer up, then opened Internet Explorer and went to LoveMatesForever.com.

I giggled, sipping through the straw and drawing in a sweet, delicious mouthful of mocha coffee. "You kill me!"

"I know, but it's a surefire way to make you laugh." Andy typed in the required search terms and drew up my brother's profile. Then, she pulled the lid off her coffee to blow lightly across the top.

"Ewwwwww," I said, pointing at the opening line of Rob's profile and fighting my gag reflex.

Single Man ISO A Real Chick

Yeah, brilliant Rob had set this one up on his own, without having me help. And it was painfully evident. My God. No wonder he was bringing hookers over to the house. As scary as Fluffykins had been, she was likely the cream of the crop who had contacted him, based on what he'd written here.

I'd hate to see some of the other women who'd been drawn to his profile.

Andy snorted as she scanned the opening line too. "Wow, that's so appealing. And flattering too. Rob wants a *real* chick this time, as opposed to the blow-up ones who won't stay hidden in the back of his closet."

At least Rob did one thing kind of right. The picture in his profile was him graduating from the police academy. It was a good, flattering shot, especially since women love men in uniforms. Not that Rob was a real man or anything, but I could see why people might think that was attractive.

"Hey, look," I said, "he cropped me and Mom out of the picture." Rob's arms, which had been wrapped around our shoulders, were chopped off the sides of the image. Nice.

"Soooo, you said on the phone that you had a saucy encounter with Derek today," Andy said, shooting me a sideways glance with one raised eyebrow. "Care to talk about it with Auntie Andy? Maybe it'll help take your mind off your parents getting their freak on."

"You suck," I said, my gag reflex threatening to give. "I'm going to hurl on you if you keep that up."

"Sorry," she said, not looking apologetic in the least.

"Anyway, the whole thing in art class was insane." In between sips of coffee, I explained the discussion between Derek and me.

"Very intriguing," Andy finally said, rubbing her chin in an exaggerated sage-like manner. "Yes, given the evidence you've presented, I definitely think he was flirting with you. The apples comment was to let you know he'd noticed you in more than a 'friendly' way. I don't think he was making fun of you at all. Don't sweat that."

"You think?" Hope fluttered anew in my stomach. Could it be true? Could I have a real chance with Derek?

"There's no doubt in my mind. He's intrigued by you, possibly because of how striking you appear in a bikini." Before I could speak, she held up her hand and cut me off. "I'm kidding, okay? But keep throwing yourself in his line of sight, and Derek will start flirting even more. That's how guys work."

"How do you know?"

"Guys are actually fairly predictable, so I know certain techniques work with them. It's just like with advertising. Keep putting a product in the forefront of your buyer's mind, and he'll remember it. Look how well it works for mops and cleaning stuff—those theme songs get stuck in your head whenever you see their commercials."

"Gee, thanks soooo much for comparing me to a mop," I said in a droll tone. "Nothing says 'I'm sexy' like washing pasta sauce stains off the kitchen floor."

"Oh, stop it. I'm telling the truth. Plus, you're not like some of those skanks at school who practically rip their clothes off in front of Derek to get his attention. You stay classy, and don't resort to stupid tricks like that. He'll see how cool you are whenever he's around you."

That was actually a good idea. If I kept myself near him more, hopefully wearing all my clothes and not babbling like an idiot during those encounters, he'd be sure to see the real me. And even better, no cupid magic would be involved.

"Thanks," I said, greatly heartened. "I think I can do that. You're full of wisdom."

"No problem. I try." Andy took a sip of her coffee, then looked back at the computer. "Oh. My. God. Check out what your brother wrote here, in the section on what he's looking for in a 'chick.'" She dropped her voice low to mimic my brother: "'Do you like long, moonlit walks on the beach?'"

"Dude, this is Cleveland in March," I interjected, biting back a laugh. "And what beach is he talking about? It's not like we're in Miami."

"'I'm looking for someone who isn't afraid to be a real woman,'" Andy continued. She looked over at me, rolling her eyes. "God, you know he totally means someone who enjoys wearing miniskirts and tank tops in the winter."

I snorted. "You called it. Hey, speaking of dating, how are things with you? I haven't heard you talk about any guys in a while."

She took a draw from her coffee, then gave a sarcastic laugh. "That's because I'm on a sabbatical from guys. They're all morons."

"Not all of them," I pointed out. "Some of them are totally awesome."

"Oh, that's right," she said, fluttering her eyelashes at me and clasping her hands in front of her chest. "Derek is oh so dreamy and super-duper *fabulous*!"

I laughed. "Andy, I will hit you if you keep that up."

"Seriously, I think Derek's great for you. And one of Maya's guys will likely turn out to be perfect for her, if she ever figures out which one she likes best. Or who's the best kisser—whatever works for her. But as for me, I'm on a break. At least for right now. I'm tired of being hit on by jerks who don't care about anything but themselves." She shrugged casually and took a drink. "Not that it stops me from looking at eye candy, though. Hellooooo, hottie." She nodded her head toward the attractive college guy, wearing a

Baldwin Wallace College sweater, walking through the door.

"I guess I can understand why you feel that way." It made me sad, though, thinking of Andy swearing off love, but after all these years, I knew how she worked. Her super pickiness in guys had her saying no to dates all the time, so it wasn't like swearing off guys right now would change her life *that* greatly.

Still, I hoped she'd come around and start wanting to give love a chance again. I didn't want to force her into a love match if she didn't want to be in one, because I respected her feelings. But that didn't mean I don't want her to have a great boyfriend eventually.

And hopefully sooner, rather than later.

Chapter 13

The first thing I noticed outside of school Tuesday morning, as I headed up the sidewalk to the front steps, was Britney, perched alone on a bench. Her head was buried in her hands, and she was crying her eyes out.

"Hey," I said to her in a gentle tone as I approached, "are you okay?" I sat on the bench beside her, my butt instantly freezing on the cold wooden seat. Ick.

At the sound of my voice, Britney sniffled loudly, lifted her head, and wiped her eyes with the back of her glove.

"I'm fine," she answered, giving me a watery-thin smile. The rims of her eyes were blood-red, and dried tear tracks streaked her pale cheeks.

She was obviously upset, but not wanting to talk, and I didn't feel comfortable pushing her into it.

"Want me to get Matthew for you?" I asked.

At my words, Britney's tears started anew. They slipped down her face, landing in large plops on her slick blue jacket. She dropped her face back into her hands.

"I d-don't know what's going on with Matthew," she blurted out, her voice muffled by her gloves. "He was supposed to pick me up for school today, but he never showed up. I tried calling him, but he hasn't answered my voice mail or text messages. I don't understand—this isn't like him."

"Maybe he's just sick?" I suggested. Digging around in garbage wasn't the most sanitary hobby around, so he could have caught some kind of bug.

She sighed, shrugging her shoulders lightly. "Maybe that's it." She didn't sound convinced, though.

Even so, if he were sick, why wouldn't he text her back? That's not the action of someone in love.

Oh, no. Maybe Matthew *wasn't* in love anymore. I quickly did the math and realized that, yup, the spell was due to wear off today. How could I have forgotten? With all the madness around Maya's love life, as well as matching up DeShawn and Marisa, hyper-analyzing Derek's every word, plus dealing with my hormone-driven parents, it completely slipped my mind.

"I'm so sorry," I said, a thread of guilt twisting around my stomach. How did this relationship fail? They'd seemed so wrapped up in each other for the last two weeks. Was Matthew really trying to ditch her? What could I do?

"I'll be fine, thanks," Britney said, sniffling again. She rose. "I'd better get to class." She shuffled away, her body hunched over.

I chewed my thumbnail, deep in thought. Maybe everything would still turn out okay. After all, it could just be a simple misunderstanding, a small fight, one that could be fixed through some effort. Even if Matthew was no longer under the love spell, he still must care for Britney a little, right? All I knew was I certainly didn't want to be responsible for Britney's heartache.

In all the time I'd been a cupid—well, these past two weeks, anyway—I hadn't considered the downside to the job: the fact that the couples I paired up might *not* stay together forever.

Once that realization hit me, it opened the floodgates, and the bad thoughts kept coming. What if *none* of the couples I'd matched up stayed in love? If Marisa dumped DeShawn, he'd probably become even more insufferable than he'd been in the first place, and even more down on romance.

What if, next week, Maya ended up alone and bitter? What if none of the guys stayed in love with her, or she ended up not wanting to be with any of them? She'd withdraw even further back into herself, and I'd never get her to go on a date again.

No, I wouldn't accept defeat. I'd make sure Maya and Britney and DeShawn ended up happy, damn it. I was a cupid, and it was my job to help people find lasting love! I was gonna see what the deal was with Matthew, and then I'd take it from there.

Feeling reinvigorated, I rushed up the walkway to school. Maya was already waiting inside the doors for me, a big smile on her face as she clutched her trumpet case. Her hair hung in light waves down her back instead of being pulled up in a ponytail, and she was wearing a light green sweater and cute low-rise jeans.

But even more important, above all the makeover changes she'd been making, she looked happy, totally oblivious to whatever fate awaited her next Monday.

No, I couldn't fail her.

"Hey, where's your morning escort?" I asked. At this point, I couldn't keep the schedule straight anymore. But since I planned it out myself, I didn't want to admit that, so I kept my words vague.

She shrugged. "Quentin had an emergency yearbook meeting, so he had to come in early. I told him I would just walk myself and see him before class."

"So, are you still thinking balloon-man Ben is 'The One'?" I asked.

"Well, I was, but then Josh and I had such a fun time hanging out last night that it made me think he's the one to choose. We're planning to go see this new horror movie next weekend." She sighed. "But then, when Quentin called to say he couldn't walk me this morning, we had the best phone conversation, and I—"

The first bell rang, interrupting her romance saga. We headed inside with the rest of the students, trying not to be jostled to death in the chaos of the hallway. Homemade posters covered the walls and lockers, courtesy of the pep squad, encouraging students to attend the basketball game at the end of the week against our rival team, Lincoln High.

"Are you ready for your big solo at the game on Friday?" I asked Maya.

She groaned, moving the trumpet case into her other hand. "Well, I've been practicing, but not as much as I should. I just haven't had time, with all the dates lately. Anyway," she said, changing the subject, "how was your evening?"

"Not bad. I read a few chapters of *Jane Ey*—ooph—" My words were interrupted as I slammed in the back of a tall guy in front of me, who'd suddenly stopped dead in the middle of the hallway.

Wobbly, the guy spun around on the balls of his feet, trying to right himself as he examined me. "You okay?" he asked in a rush. He swiped a hand across his forehead to move a strand of shaggy black hair out of his eyes.

Giving him a small nod, I tried to regain the breath that had whooshed out of me at the impact.

"Sorry about that," he mumbled. "Some girl stopped in front of me, and I didn't want to run into her. I didn't know anyone was right behind me."

"Hey," Maya said, "aren't you in my French class? You're the new guy, right?"

His cheeks turned a deep red, and he nodded.

Aw, poor guy. No wonder he was so jumpy and embarrassed. It sucked being the new kid at school. Ooh, but as a cupid, I'm the perfect person to help him out. I should try to find out more about this guy so I can start a profile in my PDA. Janet had encouraged me in our weekly meeting yesterday to keep working on new matches.

Yeah, this guy needed me, and I'd make it my job to find him the perfect love match.

"I'm okay, really," I told him, feeling generous. "No worries."

Quentin came out of nowhere just then and pushed in between me and Maya to stand in front of her. A digital camera dangled around his neck.

"Hey," he said to her, giving the new guy a glance, then dismissing him by completely turning his back to the guy. "There you are! I want to take some shots of you with the morning light. Let's plan some time tomorrow morning, okay?" He grabbed Maya's elbow and led her off toward our English class.

I turned back to the new guy, but he was gone.

With a tired groan, I sank into my seat between Maya and Andy at the cafeteria table, grabbing a bright green apple from my brown paper lunch bag. What a long day, and it was only lunchtime. I was also keeping an eye out for Matthew so I could see what was going on with his love match. The issue plagued the back of my mind, chewed at my conscience.

Yeah, I was so ready for spring break next month. Not that I was going to do anything fun. Mom wouldn't dream of letting me escape Cleveland to go somewhere south, where the sun might possibly shine more than five minutes a day.

I looked at Maya's lunch tray, glad I'd brought a PB&J sandwich and chips. There was no way I'd touch the meat loaf surprise. Ick. God only knew what lurked in those little brown loaves of doom, but I guarantee it wasn't real meat.

"You guys are coming to the game on Friday night, right?" Maya asked. "And then, sleepover at Andy's?" She picked up her fork and poked at the "meat" loaf, her nose wrinkling in disdain.

I took a bite of my apple, then said around a mouthful, "I'll totally be there." Not that I knew a damn thing about basketball, of course, but I could support my friends with the best of 'em.

"The chance to watch you seduce the rest of the school with your mad music skills?" Andy teased. "I wouldn't miss it for the world."

"Hardy har." Maya threw a balled-up napkin at Andy, who cackled evilly in response.

"Maya," Ben said, suddenly appearing beside her and me. He stared down at her, his face rapt. "Hi."

"Ben!" Maya smiled at him, then peeked at her watch, a deep

crease between her brows. "I'm . . . surprised to see you. Don't you have a different lunch period?"

She glanced at Andy and me with alarmed eyes, blinking rapidly. Apparently, it wasn't Ben's turn to eat lunch with her. Crap.

A small flash of irritation shot through me. What was it with these guys, just eating up Maya's time whenever it was convenient for them? Between Quentin's obsessive photo shoot, Josh's midnight visit, and Ben's awkward-but-cute-but-creepy locker invasion, the girl barely had room to breathe. The boys were totally not sticking to the schedule.

Maybe there was a lesson to be learned in this—I guess guys in love can't be controlled, after all. Definitely good to know for future reference.

All four of us stared at one another in awkward silence. Ben's cheeks reddened as he shuffled from foot to foot. He obviously wanted to sit down beside Maya, but I refused to move over.

Actually, I was trying my best to figure out how to nicely get him to leave, before Maya's *real* lunch date showed up. Time was of the essence here.

Andy cleared her throat. "So," she asked Ben, "you stoked about Friday's game?"

"Game?" Ben echoed, not peeling his eyes from Maya. "What game?"

Andy's eyebrows shot up clear into her hairline. "Um, the big basketball game. The one you're supposed to be announcing . . . ?"

"Oh," he said with a nervous chuckle, his flush deepening down his throat. He finally looked over at Andy, shrugging slightly. "Yeah, right, *that* game. Sure, it'll be fun." He whipped his head to look at Maya. "You're gonna be there, right?"

Geez. The old Ben always seemed so pulled together and on top of things, on or off the microphone. This new, in-love Ben couldn't even remember when the game was. Could my love spell have changed him this greatly?

As I looked at Ben, trying to figure out how to get him away from the table, I noticed Josh weaving his way through the crowd, heading straight for our table.

Oh, hell. Things were about to go from bad to worse.

"Excuse me for a sec." After putting my half-eaten apple on the tabletop, I jumped up from my seat, darting right over to Josh.

"Hey!" I said to him in my oh-crap-I'll-just-distract-him-with-my-utter-perkiness voice. "I need to tell you something urgent."

Josh peered over my shoulder, probably trying to keep his eyes on Maya. "Yeah, what is it?"

I racked my brain while continuing to block his path with my body. *Think quickly!* "It's about Maya."

That got his attention. He halted in his tracks, eyes on me. "What about her?"

"Well, Maya's nervous about her solo on Friday. Since you're a fellow musician, I figured you're just the guy to help. Have you thought about . . . making her a mix CD or something? Maybe it would inspire her and soothe her worries."

Ugh. Stupid, stupid words poured out of my mouth in a rush, but I couldn't make myself stop. I had to give the girls time to ditch Ben.

Josh tilted his head, considering my suggestion. "She does love music," he murmured, scratching his chin. "But I don't think a CD is going to be enough to show how I feel." After a long moment of silence, he snapped his fingers, then gave me a wide, excited grin. "I got it. I know just how to make her feel better. I'll go get started right now!"

Turning, he took off through the cafeteria, bursting out the double doors into the hallway.

Well, that wasn't exactly what I'd intended to do, but whatever. It worked. I headed back to the table and plopped back down in my seat. Ben had been evacuated, leaving just the three of us again.

"God, that was too close," I said, propping my elbows up on the table and leaning my head into my hands. I couldn't wait for this dating madness to be over.

Maya groaned, her brow furrowed. "Yeah, this is way crazier than I ever dreamed it could be. I can't keep it straight anymore, and I'm still no closer to figuring out which guy I like most." She bit her lower lip. "My poor day planner is jam-packed, every day, but I'm still searching for a sure sign of which guy is the right one. I seem to like them all equally—like, whichever one is right in front of me is my favorite at the time."

A horrible, sinking feeling hit me as I stared at her overwhelmed face. What had I gotten Maya into? Since none of the guys knew about each other, Maya was doing a constant juggling act. At least the spell would be over in less than a week, and Maya could make a completely clear-headed decision then.

"Man," Andy said, shaking her head, "I'm getting tired just looking at you. Maybe you should take a break from dating a bit."

"I can't. I don't know how to explain it, but whenever I think about cutting back, I just feel completely drawn back to them. It's like I'm under some kind of spell."

"Yeah, a spell of looooooooove," Andy drawled, pointing her wiggling fingers at Maya.

My heart accelerated to about five thousand beats per minute, but Maya just rolled her eyes at Andy and kept going. "I'll just make this work somehow. It's only been just over a week. I'm sure I'll be able to decide soon, and then things will be more normal. The more I see of each of them now, the faster I'll be able to choose the right one . . . right?"

The bell rang, dismissing us from lunch.

"Time to skedaddle," Maya said, sliding out of her seat and balancing her tray in one hand. "See ya after school, guys."

I dunked my apple core in the trash and shoved my chips and sandwich back in the paper bag. So much for using lunch period to occasionally eat lunch. The sacrifices I made for my career. Well, maybe I could grab a candy bar from the vending machine later.

Andy and I headed down the hall to health class, where we were talking about the importance of adequate nutrition for teen development.

I thought about my uneaten sandwich and sighed. *Yeah, tell me about it.*

Chapter 14

"There's Quentin's little photo slut," a not-so-subtle stage whisper said as Maya and I walked toward the school's front doors at the end of the school day.

We both turned in unison. There was my archenemy Mallory, surrounded by three of her tanorexic, fake-blond diva girlfriends.

All four of them were wearing matching pastel snow parkas and low-slung jeans with thick, white fuggly boots that they clearly considered cool. Their heavily made-up eyes raked over Maya, a snobbish sneer on their collective faces.

A surge of anger throbbed in my gut, and I clenched my fists at my side. "Ex-*cuse* me?" I said, hostility freely ripping through my voice as I aimed my glare straight at Mallory. "What did you just say?"

She blinked her bright blue-contact eyes at me. "I don't know what you're talking about." She turned to her friends. "Come on, let's go."

"You're not leaving without apologizing to Maya," I said, stepping in her path.

At my movement, Mallory's eyes about bugged out of her head. Then, her hot-pink lips pursed in disgust. "I'm not apologizing for anything," she spat out. "If anyone owes anyone an apology, it's you, for stabbing me in the back."

"This again, seriously?" I asked with a heavy sigh, rolling my eyes to the ceiling, "I told you, nothing happened between me and James—*two years* ago, I might add."

"That's not what I heard," Mallory said. "And my *real* friends have no reason to lie to me."

Her vapid blond shadows nodded their heads in agreement.

What the hell did they know? They only knew what Mallory told them.

Not that anyone could tell now, but during freshman year, Mallory and I were way close. We shared a bunch of the same classes, half our wardrobes, and all of our secrets as well. Between the time I spent at Mallory's, Maya's, and Andy's houses, Mom complained I was never home.

All was going great until Mallory got a bug up her butt and decided out of the blue that I wanted to steal James, her boyfriend at the time. As if I would *ever* make a move on another girl's boyfriend, let alone a close friend's boyfriend, let alone *James*.

But Mallory ditched me in an instant, without even asking to hear the truth. And then, she turned her back on Andy and Maya too, when they refused to believe her paranoid rants. Unbelievable.

She and James broke up a few months later, but I have a sneaking suspicion Mallory never got over him.

I crossed my arms over my chest. "Well, whatever you heard was wrong. I tried explaining that to you, many times."

Actually, I'd never understood her attraction to James in the first place. I always thought he was a pretty dumb guy. He was the person in class who made armpit farting sounds and laughed too loud at how clever he was. I liked to think I could hook up with someone smarter than that.

Besides, Mallory knew how I felt about Derek, and she *should* have known I would never backstab a friend.

She held up her palm at me. "I don't care, and I don't want to talk about it." She turned and scrutinized Maya, shaking her head as if she didn't like what she was seeing. "I just don't get it. Why you?"

With a parting look of disdain, she pushed between Maya and me and strolled through the front doors outside. Her airheaded posse quickly followed.

Maya remained frozen in her spot, her jaw clenched tightly. "What did I ever do to them?" she asked me through gritted teeth.

It took me several long moments to calm my blood pressure down before I could answer her. I had to seriously fight the urge to run after them and clock Mallory square in her perky stuck-up little nose.

"You didn't do anything," I finally said. "Mallory hates me because of the James thing, and she hates you for being my friend." I paused as I replayed Mallory's words in my head. "Well, and apparently they've heard about Quentin's plans to feature you in the yearbook, and their heads are exploding with jealousy."

Maya pulled the loose strap of her backpack over her arm and up her shoulder. "Come on," she said, her voice flat. She tugged on my arm and led me out the door. "Let's just go home."

I wanted to give her the "don't let them get to you" pep talk, but it was apparent by the look on Maya's face that she didn't want to say anything else about it.

We walked back to my house in total silence. Andy was going to meet us there, since she had to run home first.

I trudged beside Maya, fuming over Mallory. Ever since our big confrontation freshman year, I'd tried to just ignore her, but that didn't stop her from picking on me every chance she got. Once, she even wrote "Felicity is a slut" on my notebook when I got up out of my desk to go to the bathroom.

I squinted and sucked in a deep breath, pissed off about the past all over again.

Friends came first, period. No exceptions. That's why Maya, Andy, and I had set that cardinal rule right after the Mallory fiasco: We'd never let a stupid guy come between us, ever. And because we felt secure in that rule, we knew we could help each other with whatever dating woes hit, like Maya's current love problems.

Maya and I turned up the driveway of my house, and I keyed the door, tentatively pushing it open.

"Mom?" I hollered, hoping she and Dad weren't swinging from the chandelier or christening the kitchen counter. My poor nerves couldn't handle another incident, and I definitely didn't want to subject my friends to it.

Silence greeted us. Nobody was home.

Thank God. At least I could get a mini-break from their public displays of affection. If I had to see my dad squeeze my mom's butt one more time, I was going to lose it.

"Come on in," I said to Maya, heading over to check the answering machine. There was one message from Mom, saying she and Dad wouldn't be home until later, but would bring dinner.

"Want something to drink?" I asked.

"I guess." Maya shrugged halfheartedly, her eyes cast down as she tossed her backpack on the floor beside our living room couch.

"Hey, I know—want me to set up a hit on Mallory?" I asked, trying to make her smile again. "I'll hire someone to break her kneecaps. Actually, I bet we'd get a line of people at school offering to do it for free."

She chuckled, plopping down on the couch. "Sure, that'd be great."

I dug into the fridge and grabbed us two Diet Cokes, then headed into the living room. "Let's get down to business," I said, handing her a drink. "We got some big-time studying to do."

We spent the next half hour discussing the ins and outs of *Jane Eyre*. Mrs. Kendel had warned us she'd be giving a short-answer quiz on the book, so we wanted to be prepared.

Maya had originally been scheduled for an after-school date

with Quentin, but when I'd pushed for her to study with me, knowing that that date would mean less study time for her, she of course had followed the rule: Friends come first. Quentin could wait until later to do some nature shots of her.

A heavy pounding on the door startled me. I jumped up and answered. It was Andy, bearing snacks.

"Oh, thank God you're here," I said with a big, dramatic sigh, taking the bag. "I'm starving. I thought my stomach would start chewing on my own spinal cord."

"Funny, funny. And I'm so glad to see you too," Andy said. She slipped over to the couch and sat beside Maya, the amusement on her face disappearing as she wrapped an arm around Maya's shoulders. "Hey, I heard you guys had a big scene with Mallory and her skank-gang today after school. Everything okay?"

Maya shrugged her shoulders. "I'm fine," she mumbled.

"Geez, the rumor mill works fast." I groaned, ripping open the bag of Doritos. I popped a super-cheesy chip in my mouth, chewing fast. "She was just being a jerk, as usual. I'm sure it was her time of the month or something."

Andy drew in a short breath. "I'm not so sure about that," she replied. "The rumor mill's also churning out some trash-talking stories about Maya and her dating life. I tried to dispel them as best as possible, but gossip is flying all over the place."

Maya's mouth flew wide open. "People are talking about me? I don't get it. Why do they care?"

I plopped back down on the couch beside Andy, cramming another chip in my mouth. "Because some people have nothing better to do than make up crap about people."

Mallory was so going down for this, if it was the last thing I did.

Andy nodded in agreement. "Mallory and her clan are just pissed that Quentin's featuring Maya in the yearbook instead of showing a thousand photos of their hoochie selves."

An angry flush burned Maya's cheeks. "They can have the whole yearbook, for all I care. I just wanted to spend time with Quentin. I *so* don't need this right now."

An utterly brilliant idea came to mind, a way to make love conquer all *and* get them off Maya's back. God, I was so, so good. Call me Saint Felicitas.

"Don't worry anymore about it," I told Maya, smiling. "I'm gonna take care of this. You just focus on your solo. And figuring out your social life, of course."

She and Andy shot me curious and slightly worried looks, which I waved off.

"I won't be breaking her kneecaps, I promise," I said, laughing. "I'll just nip the rumors in the bud. She won't be talking about you any longer."

Because instead of having time to spread malicious gossip, Mallory was going to be too busy focusing on the new love of her life . . . Bobby Blowhard.

The plan was so brilliant, it was scary.

"And speaking of rumors," Andy said, leaning in, "what's going on with Matthew and that Britney girl he was dating? I heard she was crying outside of school this morning. Did he dump her?"

Maya's eyes widened. "That's awful."

My stomach flipped over as guilt clutched me in its grip again. "Yeah, it—it is." Gah! With all the lunch drama, I forgot I still hadn't seen Matthew at all today. "Have you seen him?" I asked as casually as possible. If there was any news to be had, perhaps Andy had heard something.

She shook her head. "Nope. I don't have any classes with him."

Darn.

Well, there went that idea. I made a mental note to keep digging for information on Matthew. It was almost certain their love match was a failure, though, and I dreaded talking to Janet about it next Monday. She probably wouldn't take the news too well. But I wanted to confirm it before I told her.

"Love comes and goes so quickly sometimes, doesn't it," Maya observed, shaking her head sadly.

Unfortunately, it sure did.

The next morning, Wednesday, was surprisingly warm, with temperatures breaking the fifties. Finally. I was anxious for spring to actually show itself. As I stared wistfully out the window of my English class, I almost yearned to prance around freely outside, except I knew the mud factor would be crazy gross right now, what with all the melting snow.

The quiz at the beginning of class had gone well. Mrs. Kendel showed unusual mercy and only gave us a couple of short-answer questions. And thank God, they were all from the material Maya and I had read yesterday.

So I'd finished up early and was busy mentally traipsing around outside, waiting for everyone else to be done.

"Miss Walker." Mrs. Kendel's sharp voice interrupted my

wandering thoughts. "Would you like to join us for class today in both body *and* mind?"

The smart-ass answer would be, *Yeah, right,* but considering I needed to pass her class to eventually graduate, I meekly nodded.

Other students tittered at her verbal smackdown, and I forced myself to focus the rest of class. I noticed DeShawn taking notes as Mrs. Kendel talked. Was he working on the haiku for Marisa? When the spell wore off, would he change back into his buttheaded self, or would love continue to conquer all and keep him different than he used to be?

When the bell rang, Maya and I flew out the classroom door—Maya to meet her escort to the next class (Ben this time), and me to see if the newest love match I'd made last night had worked.

As I considered the Bobby-Mallory setup, I knew a part of me should feel guilty about pairing them, but I had to be honest. I didn't feel bad at all. In fact, wasn't it selfless of me to give my worst enemy a chance at love?

And who was I to say it wouldn't work, anyway?

The profiles I'd written on Bobby and Mallory were finely crafted works of art, to be sure. I should consider becoming a novelist, given the way the words had come out of me in an almost inspired fashion. Instead of commenting on their massive egos, I'd written that both had a healthy sense of self. I also said they were both engaging conversationalists, as well as passionate about physical well-being.

Yeah, I had a gift.

Besides, all of that word-smithing was for Janet's benefit, as well, since surely she'd be scrutinizing my pairings. I'd lucked out and avoided being caught matching Maya with three guys, and Janet hadn't said anything about the e-mails I'd sent to my parents, but I wasn't about to take any more chances—this job was just too much fun, and it had way too many unexpected side benefits. Plus, having a new love match would show her I was still working hard.

I spied Bobby standing about twenty feet away, his back pressed against a locker as he scoured the halls. Suddenly, his eyes lit up, and a huge grin broke out on his face. I'd seen that smile before—it was the look he usually reserved for *me*. Wow, was it refreshing to not be the recipient this time.

"Mallory! Mallory!" he yelled as loud as possible, frantically waving his hand. "Ma-a-a-a-alloryyyyyy!"

Biting my lower lip to keep from bursting out in laughter, I ducked into a classroom doorway and watched the scene unfold.

Mallory noticed Bobby hollering—it was kind of hard to miss it, and pretty much the whole hallway stopped in stunned silence at his ruckus.

She gave her giggle-squad an apologizing shrug, then waved them away from her. "Go ahead. I'll meet you at lunch," she said.

They stared at her retreating figure with heads tilted to the side, not believing she was giving them the brush-off for Bobby Blowhard.

For once, I totally could relate to them.

"Hey," Bobby said when Mallory got there. "You know, you've been on my mind a lot lately. Um, this morning, I mean."

Hah. I bet so. The effectiveness of these love matches never failed to amaze me.

Mallory nodded enthusiastically. She briefly stared at her feet, a blush spreading across her cheeks. "Yeah, I was thinking about you, too," she replied, licking her lower lip and daring a glance at him through her eyelashes.

Bobby's pecs began their instinctive mating dance, bouncing in some kind of rhythm only he could hear. "Wanna meet me in the gym later? Maybe we could work out together," he said, eagerness pouring into his voice.

Students around them were frozen in place and openly staring, not even bothering to hide their shock. Not that I could blame them. The school's biggest snob, hooking up with Bobby? It was a tale for *Ripley's Believe It Or Not*. A few people actually giggled out loud.

Mallory ignored them all, focusing solely on Bobby. She nodded in assent and brushed his upper arm with her fingertips, smiling at him with an earnestness I hadn't ever seen in her before.

Wow, she was definitely smitten—I don't think she'd even looked at James like that, back when they were together. It was kind of weird to watch, honestly.

The bell rang. Students groaned, but dashed off to class, their whispers about Mallory whirling all around. This would definitely end any talk about Maya, since this was way juicier stuff to focus on, witnessed firsthand.

Problem? Solved. Go Felicity!

"I gotta go to class now," Mallory said in a breathy voice, waving bye to Bobby. She backed away slowly, eyes still locked on his until she bumped into an open locker door. "I'll see ya."

He watched her leave. "Bye, Mallory!" he screamed to her departing figure at the top of his lungs.

Holy crap, their relationship was going to be even better than I'd imagined.

Chapter 15

Constellations glow,

but their shine cannot compare

to your inner star.

"Wow, DeShawn," I said, utter surprise stunning me for a moment. "This is a really good haiku. Did you write this by yourself?"

DeShawn had found me lingering in the hallway after Bobby and Mallory walked off and immediately thrust his poem into my hand, grunting that he wanted me to read it.

I leaned back against my locker, rereading the scribbled poem on the crumpled-up piece of notebook paper. A part of me was sure he must have stolen it from somewhere. It sure didn't sound like the DeShawn I knew.

He nodded in response and gave me a halfhearted shrug, looking a little unsure as to whether or not to believe my compliment. "Thanks. I worked hard on it. Think Marisa will like it?"

I blinked. "She'd be an idiot not to," I blurted out, almost scoffing at the idea of her not being taken in by these romantic words. "It's fabulous."

What girl *wouldn't* be flattered by such a lovely poem? I'd practically stab someone in the face for a poem like this to be written about me.

I handed DeShawn back the piece of paper, suddenly feeling peppy and excited about his love match. At least one coupling was working out well. And thank God for that. I hadn't spotted Matthew at all since seeing Britney cry Tuesday morning, so I was unsure of what to do in that area.

DeShawn folded the paper and crammed it in his back pocket. "Gotta go. Later," he said, taking off down the hall without a care in the world.

I turned back to my locker, grabbed my American history book, and headed to my boring class, dragging my feet the whole way. On a more positive note, I now had something awesome to tell my cupid boss Janet in our Monday meeting.

She'd probably think DeShawn's love poetry was cool, too.

Then, I noticed Matthew himself, a few feet ahead of me down the hallway. He was resting a palm against the wall, leaning in close and talking to Britney. Sweet, blissful relief swept through me at the sight of the two of them together.

No, wait, that wasn't Britney. This chick had darker hair than Britney and was wearing one of those granola dresses, with brown, hemp-looking fabric. Even her dirt-brown sandals looked like you could smoke them.

Matthew laughed at something the granola girl said. He stroked the side of her face with his palm, then planted a small kiss on her forehead.

The same gesture he'd done with Britney when I'd seen them in the hallway together last week.

My stomach fell. Guess it was official. My first failed love match—signed, sealed, and flushed down the toilet.

I heard a sharp gasp from behind, and turned to see Britney stop in her tracks right beside me. She stared in horror at Matthew for a long moment, then ran into the bathroom, the heavy door closing behind her.

The bell rang, signaling it was time for us stragglers to dash into class. I shifted on my feet, unsure what to do. The love match was technically over, and it was out of my hands, but I felt horrendously guilty leaving Britney in such disarray.

After all, it was my fault for pairing the two of them in the first place.

With a light push, I gingerly headed through the bathroom doorway. "Britney?"

I heard a sniffle in the last stall. Then, Britney shoved the stall door open. "Oh, it's you," she said, blinking rapidly to clear the tears out of her eyes. "Sorry, you seem to catch me in the worst moods lately."

"I don't mean to be so nosy, but I saw you run in here. You wanna talk?" I leaned back against the sink counter.

She moved toward the sink too, then turned on the faucet and splashed water on her eyes. "Nothing to talk about, except my boyfriend and I broke up yesterday, and he's already moving on to someone—" Her words broke off with a sob.

I had a sudden impulse to hug her, but held back. We really didn't know each other all that well. Instead, I settled for nodding empathetically. "That sucks. I'm sorry to hear that."

"I guess he got tired of how different we were. I tried to be someone he wanted, but I just wasn't enough. I even dug through garbage for him even though I hated it, just because he'd wanted to." Her voice sounded bitter, even as it seemed weak and unsure. She was probably experiencing the full spectrum of emotions right now.

As for me, I had one overwhelmingly strong feeling: guilt. Britney's words about how different she and Matthew are stabbed me right in the stomach. And what's worse is that she was right. It was my job to ensure compatibility, and I messed that up royally.

I had no idea what to say to her in response.

Britney studied her reflection in the mirror, then dug into her purse to pull out concealer, dabbing it around her eyes and gently rubbing the makeup in. Her eyeballs were still red, but the eyelids didn't look so rough.

"Maybe I just need to try harder," she said. "Maybe I can win him back."

I bit my lower lip, studying her face. What would Oprah say to her right now? I tried to channel the queen of talk therapy.

"You know," I said slowly, "that might work for a while. But what happens if you 'slip up' again, even accidentally? Is it worth constantly walking on eggshells, afraid you're gonna ruin the relationship?"

"Yeah," she hedged, "but I hate to give up on something I've worked on. I feel like a quitter." She cast her eyes down, her shoulders slumped.

"But you're not a quitter. You're just being smart and getting out of something that isn't working. Even if you're giving one hundred percent of yourself into a relationship, it's still only fifty percent."

Holy crap, I was even more profound than I realized. I was really getting into this counseling stuff. It wasn't going to earn me any lasting-match bonuses, but at least I was undoing some of the damage I'd caused.

She stared at me for a moment, a light of hope flashing in her eyes. "Yeah, maybe you're right."

It was sorely tempting to pair Britney up with a new match and give her a quick romantic boost with another guy, but she needed time to focus on herself and her own needs before diving back into a relationship. I made a mental note to give it a month or so, then try to find Britney a better match.

I stood up, pushing my shoulders back. "Damn straight, I'm right! I think you should spend more time working on *you* instead of trying to get him back. Screw Matthew. Viva la independence!"

Britney nodded, a smile growing on her face. "Viva la independence," she echoed.

"You know, I haven't seen Josh in school since the lunch fiasco yesterday," I said to Maya, then took a big swig from my water bottle. After reading an article on the effects of artificial sweeteners on the complexion, I'd decided to cut my soda intake. Which was totally going to kill me, because I hearted caffeine so much, I wanted to marry it, but one had to make sacrifices for beauty.

Maya nodded. "It's all good. He texted me earlier to say he's caught up in some super-urgent project, but wanted me to know he's still thinking of me. Wasn't that sweet?" She grinned at Andy and me, then glanced at her watch. "Oh, crap, I forgot." She quickly packed up her stuff and stood. "I made a lunch appointment with Absinthia today to have my cards read."

I spat my mouthful of water all over the table. "Say what?"

Absinthia's real name is Karen Mack. She's one of those kids who cuts class like she's allergic to school, preferring to discuss poetry and the futility of life with all the other moody kids. She usually hangs out under the bleachers and smokes like a freight train.

I had no idea she did fortune-telling too, but I guess it was a better career choice than folding T-shirts at the Gap.

"She's going to read my tarot cards. Maybe her insight will help me figure out which guy is right for me." Maya looked sheepish. "It couldn't hurt, right?"

Andy rose, balling her napkin up in her fist and tossing it on her tray. She grinned madly. "Oh, no way am I missing this."

Well, I wasn't going to be the odd man out. "Count me in too." I'd never seen cards read before except on those late-night TV infomercials (*You'll soon be fifty bucks poorer, so call this number—woooooooooh*).

This would be very interesting, to say the least.

We shuffled out of the lunchroom and slipped outside, heading to the track field bleachers. Sure enough, the usual crowd was there, evidenced by the puffs of smoke rising through the seats. I heard a heated discussion going on, something about symbolism in Kafka's work.

Maya led us under the bleachers and over to the group, Andy and I on her heels. The goth kids stopped their conversation, several of them staring at us. I shuffled in place, suddenly feeling awkward.

"Absinthia," Maya said in a soft tone, "I'm sorry I'm late."

Absinthia turned, her heavily lined eyes raking over the three of us. The chains on her black wide-legged pants rattled with her movement.

"Time's relative, anyway," Absinthia said in a low voice, shrugging. She tapped the ash off her cigarette onto the ground. "Did you bring the money?"

Andy scoffed. "You're paying for this? How do you know she's even the real thing, Maya?"

Absinthia raised one eyebrow, eyeing Andy, and took a deep drag of her cigarette. "And what makes you so sure *you're* the real thing?" she said, the smoke curling out her mouth. She sneered. "At least I'm not just a product of the media conspiracy to turn teenage girls into robotic breeding machines."

One of the guys in the group nodded enthusiastically at Absinthia's words. "Exactly. Why look like every other cookie-cutter teen?"

Andy opened her mouth to reply, but I interrupted.

"Hey, this is Maya's decision," I said calmly, wanting to defuse the situation before it got out of hand. "But can we move somewhere else to do this?" I didn't want everyone and their mom staring while Maya threw her hard-earned bucks in the garbage.

Absinthia shrugged and smashed out her cigarette on the heel of her black boots, then rose, leading us back across the field and under the eaves of the school building. She plopped down at a nearby picnic table, and the three of us sat across from her. What an interesting group we must have looked like.

Maya handed her a folded bill. "Can we get started? Lunch is going to end soon."

Absinthia pulled a wrapped pack out of her large pants pocket, then unfolded her deck from the soft, blood-red fabric. She flipped through the cards and pulled out certain ones, then put the rest of them away.

"We're going to use just the major arcana deck for you," Absinthia said. "I need you to think about what your concerns are. Close your eyes and have a specific question in your mind." She shuffled the remaining chunk of cards, then put the deck down on the table. "Okay, split the deck for me."

Maya did so, and Absinthia put the two halves of the deck back together, then fanned the cards out.

"Please draw three cards," she intoned.

Maya drew in a deep breath and reached a hand out. I detected a slight shake in her fingers as she picked out three.

Absinthia flipped over the first one. "This is your past," she said, pointing to the card. "It's the hermit. You spent a lot of time inside yourself, skeptical of things around you." She shot a big grin to Maya. "A girl after my own heart. You're quite the antisocial thing, aren't you."

Maya chuckled. "Yeah, I guess that's a good way to put it."

Andy snorted. "Huh. Ya think?"

I elbowed Andy in the side, and she shot me a glare, but quieted down.

"There's nothing wrong with getting some quiet time to sort things out," Absinthia continued. She flipped over the next card, a man and woman embracing each other. "This is your present, representing the lovers. You're currently in the throes of making a big decision."

Goose bumps rose across the surface of my arms.

"Whoa," Andy breathed. "That's freaky."

Maya gasped. "Oh, that's it! But what do I do?"

Absinthia nodded knowingly. "What this card is really saying to me is that you need to follow your gut, even if it's scary. You may be led to believe there's a certain . . ." She paused, weighing her words. "A certain path that's right for you, but it may not be the one you're supposed to be on. You need to forge your own path, look at your instincts, or else you won't be complete."

"I know," Maya said with a heavy sigh. "I just don't know what that path is."

My heart went out to her. This was obviously tearing her apart. Would it have been better for me not to give her the option to choose?

"Don't the cards give her any guidance on what to do?" I asked.

"She already knows the answer, deep down inside," Absinthia replied. "She just needs to articulate it, make it happen." She flipped over the third card. "Hm," she said, pursing her black-colored lips. "This is your future. The moon card. It seems you're in for a bit of a wild ride, so get ready. There are probably going to be some ups and downs for you, but just hang in there and ride it through."

Maya groaned. "Great."

The bell rang. Time to get back inside.

I patted Maya on the back. "Hey, it could have been worse. At least you didn't get the death card, right?" I teased, slipping off the bench.

"Actually, the death card isn't the bad one. The one that causes all the troubles is the tower. That one's all about drastic upheaval." Absinthia bundled her cards back up and tucked them back into her cloth, then rose from the bench. "I gotta run."

"Thanks again," Maya said, her voice dejected. "I'll think about what you said."

Absinthia gave her another smile. "Thanks for the business," she said, then pulled out her cigarette pack, smacking the bottom to force one out the top hole. She plucked it out and headed back to the bleachers. "See ya."

Andy, Maya and I headed inside, quiet as we all considered Absinthia's words. She'd said Maya already knew what she wanted to do.

For Maya's sake, I hoped that was true.

Chapter 16

"Settle down!" Principal Massey bellowed as over a hundred juniors spilled into the auditorium bleachers that afternoon for the last period of school.

About once a month, our school held assemblies for the different classes, and today was the juniors' lucky day. The other half of our class had had their assembly the period before—unfortunately for me, it seemed Derek was with that other group. No chance for drooling over him. Boo.

Principal Massey pointed at a jock, clad in his football jersey, who was lingering in the hallway with his girlfriend and scoring some kissy-kissy time before the assembly. "Harper, get in the bleachers, sir!"

“Fiiiiine,” he groaned. Reluctantly, he gave his girlfriend a last kiss and shuffled his way in.

With the stealth of ninjas, Maya and I slipped into a crowded section, making sure there was no room around us. After the lunchtime tarot card reading, we’d decided to avoid any hints of favoritism with whichever of her guys would be at the assembly by giving them no chance to sit with us. From what I could tell by scouring the bleachers, only Ben was in here with us, and he was already parked in a seat and talking to some other guys. It was apparent he hadn’t seen us.

Whew. Fortune was on our side.

And even better, Marisa and DeShawn were right behind us, so I could oh so casually listen in on their conversations and get an idea of how their relationship was going. Sadly, I noticed Marisa’s friends were not even sitting with them, letting her and the whole class know exactly how they felt about DeShawn.

Given my rocky past with him, I could understand their hesitation to believe in the new DeShawn, but I knew better than anyone how love could change a person.

“Today, our assembly will be on sexual harassment.” Wearing low, thick black pumps, Principal Massey paced in front of the bleachers, keeping her eyes firmly on all of us. I think she was afraid that given the nature of the topic, there might be some rambunctious behavior. She was probably right.

"Mr. Johns, who works with the guidance counselor's office for our school district, will be speaking to you," she continued. "Please give him your full attention." She waved him to the front and took a seat nearby, where she could watch all of us.

"This is so going to suck," I whispered to Maya. "The guys who are the most likely to harass girls aren't going to pay any attention, anyway."

She nodded. "No kidding."

Mr. Johns stepped forward, standing in front of a large TV. He was the skinniest man I'd ever seen in my life. A stiff breeze could probably sweep him right out a window. He was clad in all black, including a black beret perched jauntily on the side of his head.

I'd never seen anyone wear a beret before. It was so bold and uncaring about modern-day conventions, it was almost hip.

Almost.

"Hello, everyone," he said, his mouth splitting into a huge grin. The gap between his front two teeth looked big enough to drive a car through. "Thanks for coming to the assembly today. We're going to be discussing sexual harassment, which means unwanted sexual advances toward the victim. Does anyone know some of the dif-ferent types of harassment?"

The room was silent. I heard a few under-the-breath mumbles between DeShawn and Marisa, but I couldn't understand what they were saying. I shifted in my seat, trying to lean a bit closer. Casting a quick glance over my shoulder, I saw their hands clasped together and their heads leaned in close.

Aw, how cute! They really did make a great couple.

Mr. Johns took our silence in stride. "Well, there's one kind where someone in power harasses a victim. It may be a teacher, a coach, or even one of the administrators."

I heard someone whisper, "Like who, Massey? Right." A couple of people chuckled.

Principal Massey cleared her throat and sat straight up, her slitted eyes scanning the crowd to see who was talking.

"Anyway, that person in charge would use his or her power to sexually harass someone," Mr. Johns continued, his voice boisterous and absurdly perky, considering the subject matter. "Another kind is a hostile environment, meaning the victim would be in an environment that was threatening. Harassment isn't just touching. It can include inappropriate words, looks, or behaviors that are unwanted. I've brought in a video that I think will help show you what harassment is and how you should handle it."

Principal Massey rose and shut off the lights. Mr. Johns clicked the large TV on, then pushed in the video tape. The fact that it wasn't a DVD filled me with a sense of dread. This was not going to be fun.

After fast-forwarding for a minute, he let the video play, stepping to the side and turning up the volume.

A narrator's deep voice boomed through the auditorium, and a bunch of us jumped at the startlingly loud sound.

"Meet Jane!" the narrator proclaimed. On the screen flashed the image of a teen from what had to be the nineteen seventies. She was wearing plaid bellbottom pants, and the neckline of her pastel blue shirt had exaggerated collar points that I thought until now was just a costume effect for hippie outfits.

Jane strolled down the hallway, her long brown hair swishing behind her as she waved at people. She reminded me of Marcia Brady from *The Brady Bunch.* Jane stopped in front of her locker. A jock, bearing helmet hair and a smarmy smile, swaggered up behind her.

"Jane's your average teenage girl. She's hip, and she likes to have a good time."

I heard several snickers from around me. "Yeah, I heard that about her," one guy said.

Maya giggled at the comment. "I don't think this video is working," she whispered to me, shaking her head.

The narrator continued, "Bradley also likes to have fun, but Bradley is about to make a big mistake."

Bradley sidled up to Jane's side. "Hey, there, groovy chick," he purred, rubbing his hand up and down her arm.

Jane froze, her face an exaggerated mask of horror. "Bradley, I'm not comfortable with that," she said. She turned to face the camera as the scene around her froze. "But what do I do about it?"

I couldn't bite back a snort of laughter. Was this for real?

"Pay attention," the principal barked to our group. In return, there were several loud chuckles.

I heard Marisa whispering, "They won't even turn around and say hi." Her voice sounded low, broken.

Instantly, I sobered up and tried to block out the sounds of the stupid video. The friend situation was getting worse for her, and it seemed like it could cause real trouble.

"What's their problem?" DeShawn said. "I'm tired of being judged by those bit—"

I heard Marisa draw in a quick breath.

"Sorry," he mumbled, sounding sincere. "I know they're your friends. I just hate how they act."

My stomach tensed. If DeShawn didn't keep himself in check, Marisa might finally listen to her friends and dump him when the spell wore off next week. She might be in love with him now, but I knew all too well how that could disappear in the blink of an eye.

I turned my attention back to the video, all the while trying to figure out if there was anything I could, or should, do.

"Omigod, thank you guys sooooo much for this," Maya said, kissing me and Andy quickly on the cheek and giving us chips and drinks. "Here are some snacks, on me."

After the junior assembly, which Principal Massey had ended early due to the exponentially increasing heckling, Ben had finally spotted Maya and asked her if they were still on for tonight's date at the bowling alley. Maya had agreed, but later asked if Andy and I could come and spy on one last date. She wanted us to help her see if Ben was the guy she was supposed to choose, especially since we'd already observed her dates with Quentin and Josh.

There was a pool table at the bowling alley. And where there was pool, there were cute college guys for Andy to scope out. So of course, we were glad to help.

"Go have fun," Andy said, shooing Maya away from our spot. She crammed a chip in her mouth. "We'll watch and give our professional diagnosis. Ben's not supposed to know we're here, anyway. Don't give us away!"

Maya flitted over to Ben, who was tying on a pair of rental shoes. She gave him a kiss on the cheek.

"They really do look cute together," I said, snaking a chip from the tray. "Then again, she looks cute with Quentin and Josh too. I don't know how she's going to choose one."

"I know." Andy and I watched as Maya showed Ben the right way to hold the ball. Following her lead, he released it down the lane and knocked over eight pins. She hugged him tightly, giving him a big smile.

"They all seem like good guys," Andy said. "If I were her, I'd just keep dating them all. Why not? You get three times the love and attention."

"You would not," I scoffed, rolling my eyes. "You won't even date *one* guy, much less three."

"Good point." She took a drink of her soda. "Anyway, my mom would choke me if I brought that many guys around. 'None of those boys are good enough for you!'" Andy said in a high, perky voice, mimicking her mom.

"Well, you *are* quite a catch," I said, waggling my eyebrows at her.

Even though I was teasing, it was true. Andy was gorgeous and fun, and I hoped she'd give love another chance soon. She deserved to be happy.

"Enough about me. Let's focus on Maya," she said, shaking her head at me with a chuckle.

Observing Maya with Ben showed us a lot. She really was different with him than she was with the other guys—quiet, but with a steady sort of confidence.

"Hey there," a large man holding a cue stick said, interrupting us as he came over to Andy. He had to be almost as old as our parents. And even better, he sported a mullet that flowed down his back in delicate ringlets. I'd never seen such carefully coiffed hair in my life. "You wanna play a game with me?"

I felt a shudder ripple through me. Any kind of game this guy wanted to play would probably result in him doing some jail time.

"No, thanks," Andy said, giving him a polite smile and turning her attention back to Maya.

Pervy Mullet Man turned his attention to me. "Well, what about you?"

Gee. As sorely tempted and flattered as I was to be chosen second, I was going to have to pass. "No, thanks."

"Come on," he said, thrusting the pool cue toward us. "It'll be fun. I'll even pay for the first game."

"We're busy," Andy said, no longer smiling. "Bye." She stared hard at him until he broke eye contact, shrugging his massive shoulders.

"Whatever," he said, sidling away and mumbling under his breath.

"God, what a creep. Thanks for sending him off," I said to her. Andy was good for that, though—she wasn't afraid to tell it like it was.

"I think Jane, the Sexual Harassment Hippie, would have had a few choice words to say to him," she said. "She would have sent his groovy self packing."

I chuckled. "Yeah, we should have taken our lead from her."

Mini crisis averted, we turned our attention back to Maya and Ben. After a few minutes of studying their body language and discussing it with Andy, we saw Ben digging in his coat pocket, proudly handing a gift over to Maya.

Her eyes widened in surprise, and she quickly tore the wrapping off. It was a Magic Eight Ball.

"Whoa," Andy said. "Now that's uncanny. Especially since she just saw that psychic chick at lunch."

"No kidding," I breathed. I had to admit, I was a little freaked out.

Maya seemed to be experiencing the same sense of shock. She stared at the gift, her mouth in a perfect O shape.

Ben nodded, saying something to her.

Maya squeezed her eyes shut and tilt the ball over, shaking it from side to side, then righted the ball and looked.

I had a feeling I knew what she'd asked. And judging by the fallen look on her face, she didn't get the answer she'd wanted.

After a couple more rounds of bowling, Maya kissed Ben good night and came back into the billiard area to do a post-date report.

"Wellllll," Andy drawled, "it was a good date. He seems really into you, and whenever you were talking, his attention was solely on you. Totally sweet."

"And you know," I interjected, "it was also totally crazy that he gave you a Magic Eight Ball. So what did you wish for?"

"Of course, I wanted to know if he was The One. Know what the message said?" Maya paused dramatically. "'Ask again later.'"

I giggled, shaking my head. "Figures."

"Even if the ball didn't help give me any good answers, I had a great time with him," she said, biting her lower lip as a happy flush spread across her cheeks. "He's not a bowler, but he's always willing to push outside his comfort zone for me. I just adore that about him."

I peeked at my watch, stifling a yawn. I was so lame, but I hadn't been sleeping well lately due to my parents, the make-out bandits. "Maybe you can sleep on it and get some clarity tomorrow. And the Magic Eight Ball may have some better answers then too," I teased.

"Good idea." She hugged us both. "Thanks again, guys. I owe you."

"You sure do. We got hit on by a guy with an Ape Drape, and it was *not* pretty," Andy said.

"*You* got hit on. *I* got your leftovers," I said, giggling. "Not that I wanted his attention or anything, though."

We gathered up our stuff and headed to Andy's car. During the drive, she and Maya dissected every minute of the date to see if they could find any signs that would illuminate a clear path for Maya. The fact that Ben had given her an eight ball was the closest thing they'd seen to a "sign." But since the eight ball didn't give an answer to Maya's question, nothing was totally clear yet.

I sat in the back, quietly remembering Absinthia's words about Maya being in for a rocky ride. Hopefully, with me and Andy helping, those rocky times would be fast and relatively painless. After all, there was no way we'd let our friend get hurt or let down.

I perked up a bit at the thought and joined in their conversation, ready to push these worries out of my mind once and for all.

Chapter 17

A whisper of a giggle slipped under my bedroom door, and I groaned in misery, glancing groggily at my alarm clock. Twelve thirty in the morning.

God, were my parents at it *again*? What were they, rabbits?

This was getting old, fast. Every time they had a moment together, they were all over each other. It was good for their relationship, sure, but bad for my beauty sleep.

I grasped for my iPod on my bedside table and popped in the earbuds to block out the sounds of *amour*, pressing the iPod on and cranking up the first song that I found. Every night since I'd love-matched my parents had been like this. They had to be taking some kind of uppers to make it through each day, given how little sleep they were getting. Totally gross.

I'd planned to get good rest, since we'd probably not get a wink of sleep during our sleepover at Andy's after the game tomorrow night. So much for that idea.

With a huff, I sat up in bed, put the iPod on my bedside table, and headed to my computer desk. If I wasn't going to sleep, at least I could update my poor, neglected blog. I turned the PC on, then hopped on the Internet and set the blog post to private diary entry.

I feel like I'm surrounded by weirdos, and it's all my fault. My parents keep copping a feel on each other, Maya's turning to psychics for dating advice, and Bobby Blowhard won't stop doing these crazy romantic gestures for Mallory.

Today at school, I walked by the gym and saw her proudly wearing a headband he'd embroidered his name onto. Yes, I said embroidered.

It was the craziest thing I've ever seen.

I snickered at the memory of Mallory's blond hair pinned to her head by the homemade pale blue sweatband. And just to make things complete, he'd even given her matching wristbands. How thoughtful.

She was probably going to regret wearing those when the spell was over, because I doubted her friends would let her live it down, ever. I hoped Quentin had snapped a photo to preserve it for posterity in the yearbook.

I chewed on my thumbnail, then continued typing.

I'm worried I made a big mistake pairing Maya up with three guys at the same time.

Maybe this was why Janet warned me not to matchmake like this. Because it's hard enough to make love work with one other person, much less three.

At least the spell will be ending on Monday, and things will finally calm down.

I hope.

I loaded the entry up and closed out of the Internet browser. With a quick push of a button, I turned the computer off, then crawled back into bed and tucked the pillow firmly over my head.

Things were finally quieter in the house, and I needed to be prepared for whatever awaited me tomorrow.

"Where's Maya?" Josh panted on Friday morning, gripping my upper arm to stop me from heading into American history. He looked like a mad scientist or a crazy Mozart-wannabe, his hair wild and spiky, his eyes about bugging out of his head. "I finally finished it, and it's amazing!"

I twisted my arm out of his grip as gingerly as possible. "Finished what?"

"Never mind." His eyes scoured the hallway. "I need to find Maya. She'll understand."

"I think she's already in class. Maybe you can catch her when it's over," I answered, studying his eyes to make sure he wasn't on drugs. I thought I read somewhere that people addicted to crack had different-sized pupils.

Josh's pupils, fortunately, seemed okay.

"Yeah, maybe." He tapped a finger on his chin. There was ink all over his hand, and it left a smudge on his face. "No, wait. I have a better idea. Okay, don't tell her you saw me. I'll surprise her tonight, instead."

I had no idea what he meant, but given how odd he was acting, it was probably better to go along with it. "You got it," I said in a soothing tone. "Mum's the word." I pretend to zip my lips.

"Good. This'll be our little secret," he whispered with a quick, conspiratorial wink, then took off running down the hallway.

What the crap was that all about?

I shook it off and went into social studies, where Mr. Shrupe was walking up and down the aisles, putting sheets of paper face-down on our desktops.

My stomach lurched, and I mentally smacked my forehead. Oh, no, a stupid pop quiz! And I hadn't done the required reading last night.

I slipped into my desk and flipped the quiz over, analyzing the questions closely. Part multiple guess, part short-answer. Maybe I could fake my way through enough to pass.

Right off the bat, question number one stumped me. So I picked C for the answer. I progressed through the rest of the first half of the quiz in a similar fashion, trying to mix it up a bit whenever I didn't know the answer.

When I got to the short answer portion, I tried to bluff my way through, making sure in the last question to also compliment

Mr. Shrupe on his choice of a lovely blue tie today. I figured a little butt-kissing couldn't hurt.

After a half hour, we handed up the tests and moved on to discussing something-or-another. Yeah, bad me, I wasn't paying much attention. Instead, I tried to push the imminent F I was sure to get out of my mind and focus on work instead.

If I could do it all over again and match Maya with just one guy from the start, which of the three would I choose? Honestly, I still wasn't sure which guy was right for Maya. Maybe Quentin? He was definitely enraptured by her, what with the constant photographs and the poem he wrote. But then again, Ben was super sweet with her, and always seemed willing to try the things Maya loved, like bowling or sushi. And Josh . . . he'd shown up at her window at midnight, and obviously was planning some big surprise for tonight.

I just hoped Maya would make the decision that was best for her. Absinthia's prophetic words wouldn't leave my mind, and I bet they were weighing on Maya too. Tonight at the game was the first time all three of Maya's suitors would be in the same room at once, and I had a feeling that would be interesting, to say the least.

I slogged my way through to the last period of the day and then headed to art class, heart in throat as usual in excitement of seeing Derek. I think I'd die if he knew how strongly he affected me. Could he see it in my eyes?

Art class went by fast. I completed carving my square of linoleum, the woman's profiled face as good as I could make it, then got the roller, ink, and paper out to start making some prints. And all the while, I peered at Derek, studying the features that were by now as familiar to me as my own.

The small freckle below his index finger knuckle. The light blond strands of color streaked through his hair—earned the old-fashioned way, through outdoor activity. The set of his strong shoulders. The light creases around his mouth when he smiled. Everything about him was just amazing, and he seemed oblivious to it. Which made him even more amazing, in my opinion.

Derek's eyes suddenly connected with mine. My heart squeezed hard in my chest at the unexpected eye contact. I tore my gaze away, embarrassed at having been busted.

Stupid! I chastised myself. *Way to be subtle there, Felicity. Why not just fling yourself across his body and beg for him to love you, while you're at it?*

The bell rang, and I gathered up my project, crammed it in the art shelf, then ran toward the door. It was time to escape with whatever dignity I had left. But of course, Derek was standing to the left just inside the doorway, talking with a couple of jocks.

"Yeah, I'll be at the game tonight," he said to them. "Should be a good one. I wanna see that guy Greene get crushed by our defense."

The other guys nodded. "We've really brought our game this year."

Oh, geez. Even as my stomach fluttered in excitement, I dragged in a pained breath. It was going to be hard to focus my attention on Maya, knowing Derek would be there.

I pushed through the door and plodded down the hallway to the front doors of the school, chewing my lower lip as I pondered another tortured night of Derek-gazing. This was getting pathetic.

Wait a minute. I squared my shoulders. I was a professional cupid, damn it! Maya and my other matches were my priority, not my hots for Derek. I needed to stop this, now.

An arm looped through mine. It was Andy, wearing her customary grin to greet me.

"Hey, hottie," she said. "Maya's practicing her solo, so she won't be walking with us."

"Oh, that's right."

We proceeded down the school steps toward my house.

"How's your job going, by the way?" Andy asked, sliding a sideways glance at me. "You never talk about it. Do they have you matchmaking anyone yet? Helping beer-bellied forty-year-old truckers find true love?"

How was the job going? I had a wild urge to tell Andy everything, from Britney to Maya to DeShawn to Mallory. Even the part about my icky parents. It would be such a relief to dish the whole saga to my best friend, to solicit her support and advice. But of course, I couldn't. I had an oath and all that.

Instead, I offered her a casual shrug. "Actually, I've been moved into the invoicing department. I have a knack for numbers, I guess."

Andy snorted. "You, loving math? Wow, that's . . . surprising. And what are things like at the office? Any crazy coworkers or hot guys? Anything good you can dish on, or is it all boring stuff?"

I said the first words that came to mind. "Well, the only thing big going on around there is the impact of the constant postal rate increases. Let me tell you, it's getting ridiculous to mail stuff out anymore."

I saw the exact moment in my reply that Andy zoned out, her eyes glazing over.

"Oh, that's nice," she mumbled.

Heartened by her bored response to my fake rant, I continued, pouring enthusiasm into my voice. "Do you have any idea how many one-cent stamps I've had to purchase? Or how many customers have sent mail to us that we had to pay on because they didn't attach the appropriate postage?"

It was an inspired performance, really. One worthy of an Oscar. But a small part of me flinched on the inside, knowing I was lying to everyone around me. And what was worse, I was getting better at it.

I wasn't sure if that was bad or good. Maybe a little of both, truth be told.

"Yeah, that's great." By the droll tone of her voice, I could tell Andy wouldn't be bugging me about my job anymore.

Another tiny crisis averted.

That night, Andy and I nestled into our seats on the school's worn wooden bleachers, scoping the crowd to see who was coming to the game. It was a nice turnout of students, parents, and members of the community, and the bleachers were filling up fast. Nearly every student in attendance, including me and

Andy, wore our school spirit shirts—the one with our mascot, the Greenville Cougar, plastered across the front.

I instantly did a Derek check, trying to see if he was here yet without being disgustingly obvious. After a couple of minutes, I saw him stroll through the double side doors, a plastic bowl of nachos in one hand and a large drink in the other. He headed to the opposite end of our bleachers and blended into the crowd, out of my line of vision.

My heart did its usual pitter-patter, and I tore my eyes away from his direction.

Okay, fine, you saw him, I admonished myself, heat tingling my cheeks. *Now, get over it.*

A guy whose face looked a little familiar moved past me to sit in the upper bleachers behind us, holding a slice of cheese pizza and a large bottled water. Oh, wait. He was the guy I ran into in the hallway . . . literally! I made a mental note about his food choices so I could add it to his profile, once I finally learned his name.

"Hey, check it," Andy leaned in close and said, "there's Maya."

Carrying her trumpet, Maya filed in with the rest of the pep band and slipped into her assigned seat with the band, in the bottom left corner of the bleachers. She looked around and, when she spotted the two of us, she waved.

We waved in response, blowing her goofy air-kisses, and Maya winked, then turned her attention back to the band director, who was getting the band warmed up.

The cheerleaders lined up in two rows on the floor right in front of Andy and me, waving their pom-poms like mad.

"Let's go, Cougars!" they cried out in unison, several of them jumping up into air splits to touch their toes. "We've got the spirit! We're number one!"

Andy turned to me and made an overly perky face. "Like, omigod, let's totally go, guys!" she cried out, pointing her index and middle fingers in the air. "We're number two, y'all! Rah rah rah!"

The head cheerleader shot Andy a glare, tossing her head in a disdainful whoosh that sent her ponytail swirling. Whoops, she must have overheard Andy being a smart-ass.

In a loud voice, the cheerleader said, "Okay, guys, everyone repeat after me!"

I tuned her out, instead watching as the two basketball teams filed onto the court to throw some practice hoops on each side of the court. I tried not to roll my eyes too hard at the self-pimping going on, what with the muscle flexing and extremely far hoops.

Ugh, snoozeville. I hate basketball so much.

At least things in boyland were going smoothly so far. Since each of Maya's guys would be handling different facets of the basketball game (Ben announcing, Quentin snapping photos, and Josh playing in the band), and Maya would be occupied playing in the band, we figured things should stay level.

Matthew and Granola Girl passed by us to sit on a bleacher between us and the band. They were holding hands, looking like two hippie peas in a pod. I felt a little dumb that I'd actually thought he'd be good with Britney, since clearly Granola Girl is exactly the kind of girl he should be dating.

Britney, I noticed, wasn't in sight—I guess she decided to give the game a pass. Well, she really was better off without Matthew. When she was ready to date again, I was totally going to find the perfect guy for her.

A weird, screeching feedback sound nearly split my head in two as the microphone in the announcer's booth turned on, and then Ben's booming voice rang through. "Good evening, everyone, and welcome to the playoff game between Greenville High and Lincoln High."

I noticed Maya beaming at the sound of Ben's voice. She gave the announcer's booth a small wave.

Applause filled the room, and the basketball players for both teams shuffled off the court onto the sidelines.

A rustling sound crinkled over the microphone, like maybe Ben shuffled some papers. "I'd . . . like to take a minute to thank Parma Pizza for the concession food available for purchase at tonight's event."

More polite applause. Then, Ben cleared his throat and said, "And one last thing. Let's all give a big hand to our Greenville High pep band. Most notably, Maya Takahashi, who is playing a trumpet solo tonight."

Andy and I jerked our heads over to Maya, whose face grew as red as a beet. Maya sank down in her seat, staring at her trumpet. As much as she liked Ben, I knew she was mortified because of the sudden attention being aimed at her.

From out of nowhere, flash after flash of camera shots from Quentin's camera bombarded Maya. "Hey," I heard him say, zooming in on her with his monster-huge lens, "Lift your face, Maya. I can't get a good shot!"

Poor Maya bit her lower lip and looked up as Quentin continued his shots. She looked utterly embarrassed, and I couldn't blame her.

Then, the double doors to the gymnasium flew open, and Josh barreled through and made a beeline for the band, looking like he hadn't slept in a year and a half. His shirt was rumpled beyond belief, and I swear he had a twelve o'clock shadow. In his hand, he clutched a pile of papers.

My stomach sank in dismay. Crap, I'd forgotten about his surprise for Maya.

I had a sneaking suspicion that maybe tonight wasn't going to go as smoothly as we originally thought.

Chapter 18

The first quarter started with a loud buzzer. Andy and I quickly started our crowd-scoping, since we lost interest in watching the game about three minutes into it. There's only so many times I can watch people run back and forth across a court before I get severely bored.

"Oh my God, look," Andy said, tugging on my sleeve. "It's Bobby Blowhard, and he's with Mallory!"

I almost choked on my drink when I saw Mallory and Bobby walk in together, bearing nachos and drinks. They were wearing matching purple muscle shirts, though at least Mallory wore a tank top under hers. She led Bobby toward her group of friends, just a couple of rows down from us.

"Hey, girls," she said to them, beaming. "Sorry we're late. We came straight from the gym." She and Bobby sat down beside them, and with her now ever-present sweat band, she wiped a bead of sweat from Bobby's brow.

"Thanks, babe. You hungry?" Bobby asked Mallory. "You should try taking in some calcium after that killer workout." He held up a cheese-laden nacho and fed it into her mouth.

She opened wide for the chip, then sucked on one of Bobby's fingers as it passed her lips. "Mmmm, delicious," she mumbled around his finger.

Her friends stared at the two of them like Mallory had sprouted an eyeball in the middle of her forehead. And the hostile, horrified looks they were throwing Bobby were even worse.

Not that Mallory noticed. She preferred to gaze soulfully into Bobby's eyes as he twitched his chest muscles at her beneath his shirt. Honestly, the sleeves had been cut back so deeply, I could see his armpit hair sprouting out from under his arms, like he had two midgets in a headlock. Nice.

Andy shook her head. "I thought I'd seen everything, but Mallory and Bobby? That's the weirdest. Can you imagine the children those two would make together? They'd never do anything but exercise and stare at themselves in the mirror."

I snorted at her description and smirked at my successful revenge. "Love knows no boundaries, I guess."

The buzzer sounded, ending the first quarter, and our side of the auditorium broke out in cheers. I guess we were winning or something.

"Go, Greenville High!" Ben said over the loudspeaker. "Ladies and gentlemen, let's hear it for trumpet player Maya Takahashi and the rest of the pep band! They're doing a marvelous job, aren't they?"

With his words, the pep band started to play the school fight song.

We all cheered along, saying our rah-rahs at the appropriate times. The song ended, and I saw Josh stand up, handing out papers to the band members. He took his place by the band director, whispering in her ear for a moment. She raised one eyebrow, skepticism written all over her face, but nodded her head.

"Hey," I said, nudging Andy. "I think Josh is up to something."

"This song is dedicated to someone special," I heard Josh say to the band. "Someone who needed a little extra . . . inspiration tonight. This one's for you, babe," he said directly to Maya, winking at her.

Josh raised his hands in front of the band and began to conduct.

A soft flute melody floated over to us, and then the clarinets started. Soon, the whole band was chiming in, their volume rising and falling with his gestures.

Maya stared in shock and awe at Josh, utterly surprised by the song he'd written for her.

And oh God, was it sappy. I think I got diabetes just from listening to the sugar-laden melody. It sounded like cheesy elevator music. The old people in the crowd were eating it up, though, their wrinkly hands clapping out of rhythm with the song.

Andy shook her head, grimacing in mock horror. "Oh no he didn't."

"Yessss," I exhaled, scrunching my face up in misery. "Yes, he did."

This must have been the big secret he'd wanted to spring on Maya. Well, I guess it could have been worse. At least it was just a song, right? And most of the auditorium didn't know that Maya was the inspiration for the crappy sap. I mean, he could have streaked across the court with "I love Maya" written on his buttcheeks.

After what seemed like two hundred years, the music finally finished, the dying strain of a tuba an odd, jarring ending. The parents and grown-ups in the crowd applauded heartily. Most students, however, didn't bother with manners, instead snickering and whispering among themselves, or even laughing outright.

The basketball game continued, and Josh headed over to quickly talk to Maya. While she was still covered in a full-face blush, I could tell she was thanking him by the nodding and smiling.

The other team's coach asked for a quick time-out, and the band director leaped up to guide the pep band in more upbeat songs. Josh dashed from Maya over to her, talking in her ear again as she conducted. She shook her head *no*, and he waved the sheet of music in her face, pointing at it.

Oh God, was he asking her to play the love song again? Surely one time was more than enough.

The band director ignored him and led the band in "Hang on Sloopy," the tune played in every high school and college sports game in the entire state of Ohio. Everyone stood and sang O-H-I-O in the appropriate spots, except for Josh, who plopped down in his seat and stared straight ahead, jaw clenched tightly.

"Wow, look at Josh. He looks pissed," I said to Andy.

She nodded. "That didn't go well."

The band took a break, and the band director headed over to talk to a group of teachers lingering by their side of the bleachers.

One of our basketball players faked left, but got tripped up trying to dodge someone, and wiped out. He held his ankle and grimaced as the refs blew their whistles and the coach ran on to the court.

The players all huddled around the injured guy. Andy and I strained to see what was going on. And then, I blinked in surprise as the audible strain of flute music started up from the band. Josh's love song, again?

Half the crowd turned its attention back to the band, including Mallory and Bobby, who actually seemed to *like* the music. Their arms were locked around each other's sides as they swayed to the sound. I heard a few kids around me make gagging noises.

"They're playing this again?" some guy behind me grumbled loudly. "Come on, play the fight song. This ain't prom, it's a basketball game!"

"This is bad," Andy groaned, smacking her forehead. "I wonder if Maya's digging it. I can't see her face right now."

I stared in horror and embarrassment as I watched Josh, guilt twisting in me. I couldn't believe he was conducting Maya's song again, and it was totally my fault because of the love spell. He was trying his darndest to woo her, but wasn't he going to get in trouble for—

At that moment, the band director realized what was happening and thundered up to the pep band's bleachers, stopping the music dead in the middle of the wobbling flute solo.

"You're done," she shouted to Josh in disgust. "Get out of here."

Josh shot one last, lingering look at Maya before stomping away from the pep band, still clinging to his magnum opus. His eyes flared with heat, and he looked like he would spit fire any second.

I popped out of my seat. "Come on," I said to Andy, pulling her up with me, "we need to get Josh to chill out before he does something even more rash."

"I'm with ya," she said, her voice filled with worry.

We wove our way down through the bleachers and caught up with our target.

"Hey," I said, grabbing his elbow, "why don't you sit with us? There's room." With my free hand, I pointed up at the bleachers.

Josh exhaled heavily through his nostrils, which flared wide open. "I guess."

"Plus, it's a pretty good view of Maya," I said.

With that, he seemed to perk up. "That won't be so bad, then."

We ushered him up there and parked him in the middle between us. He stared dead ahead, and I could hear his molars grinding in his clenched mouth.

"Hey," I said perkily, trying to distract him, "your song was great."

"You think so?" he mumbled.

"Absolutely!" I shot a look at Andy behind Josh's back, mentally encouraging her to talk it up too.

"Ohhhh, riiiiiight," Andy drawled, nodding in an exaggerated manner. "Yeah, it was amazing. I know Maya was so moved."

He rubbed his jaw, and his shoulders visibly relaxed as he pondered our flattering words. "Yeah, I guess she was, wasn't she." He shot a glare at the band director. "Too bad I was cut off so rudely."

"Oh, I know," I said in a soothing voice. He was still irritated, but the edge of his anger was vanishing. Thank God. The last thing we needed was him causing a scene. Again.

The buzzer rang, and the cheerleaders flooded the floor as the basketball players left. They performed a dance routine, flashing their bloomers every two seconds as they kicked their legs impossibly high into the air. Once the routine was done, they waved their pom-poms and danced off the floor.

The loudspeaker crackled, and Ben's voice came through. "Greenville High, in the lead at the halftime break." He cleared his throat, and I heard his voice shake. "And now, we have a special treat for you. The lovely and talented Maya Takahashi is going to perform her trumpet solo. Everyone, please give your undivided attention to this gifted star musician."

I rolled my eyes. God, could he lay it on thick.

En masse, the whole crowd turned to the band. Josh tensed beside me as he stared, unblinking, at the object of his love. Quentin, standing in front of the band, snapped about four billion shots of Maya.

The band director waved for Maya to rise. Maya stood from her seat, her hands slightly shaking. With the trumpet's mouthpiece pressed to her lips, she took a deep breath.

"Wait!" Ben's voice cried out over the microphone, bouncing off the auditorium walls. "Before you play, Maya, I just had to say in front of everyone that . . . I love you. IIIIII looooove youuuuu!"

The crowd gasped and stared at Maya, who dropped her trumpet in surprise. A loud *clang* echoed throughout the room as her instrument hit the bleacher and fell to the floor.

Beside me, Josh froze, his body becoming like a brick.

"What did he just say?" Josh spat out.

Andy and I exchanged glances. "Uh-oh," she whispered.

He jumped up from his seat and shouted, "Did he just say he loves Maya?" With a quick spin, he ran up the bleachers to the announcer's booth.

OhGodohGodohGod. My stomach flipped over itself, and I just knew I was going to hurl all over the people in front of me.

"Andy," I said frantically, tugging on her sleeve, "we have to stop him!"

"What are we going to do, jump on him?" Andy rubbed her scrunched-up brow with her fingertips. "What a nightmare."

Maya stood in place, still looking stunned. Her eyes pleaded with me and Andy to help.

"Fight! Fight! Fight!" students around us chanted, thrusting their fists in the air.

Great. Josh was going to beat the living crap out of Ben, and it was all because of my wishy-washy matchmaking.

Before I could blink, I saw Quentin book it at breakneck speed up the bleacher, hot on Josh's heels. Oh, of course—because two guys fighting wasn't going to be enough drama for the evening.

I whipped around to follow the two of them up to the booth, ignoring Andy's light grip on my shoulder to keep me in place. This was my responsibility, and I needed to think fast on how to fix it.

"Guys!" I panted as I wove in between people, reaching for the back of Quentin's shirt. "Guys, stop. Hold. On!"

I got to the booth just in time to hear Josh say, loud enough for everyone to hear over the loudspeaker, "What the hell are you doing, telling my girl you love her?"

"Your girl?" Ben squinted his eyes in confusion. "Who's your girl?" He turned off the loudspeaker.

"What? Maya, of course," Josh answered, his voice scathing. "Who else would I be talking about?"

"Why are *you* two talking about Maya?" Quentin butted in, a sneer on his face.

"Guys," I said, stopping to drag in several short, ragged breaths into my starved lungs before continuing. "Let's talk. For a second. Everyone. Just stay. Calm."

All three ignored me, as did the crowd, still chanting for a fight.

"Back off, man," Josh said, slitting his eyes at Ben and Quentin. "She's mine."

"Like hell," Quentin said, taking the camera off from around his neck and placing it on the announcer's table. "She's mine!" In the blink of an eye, he smashed his fist hard into Josh's face.

Josh's head jerked backward from the blow.

The crowd nearest us, seeing the blow, gasped in unison. Then, people burst into a furious uproar, voices buzzing all around us.

Oh, no! Oh no, oh no, oh no, this can't be happening. I tried to step in the middle of the three of them, but someone tugged on the back of my shirt.

"Felicity, don't!" Andy said from behind me. "Stay back, or you'll get hit!"

Josh touched his nose gingerly as a thin stream of blood trickled out. He pulled back his fist to hit Quentin, but Ben grabbed Josh's arm.

"She's mine!" Ben yelled. "No fighting over her!" With closed eyes, he started swinging blindly at both Quentin and Josh, his hands glancing off the sides of their heads.

From out of nowhere, a swarm of teachers and parents rushed the announcer's booth, and the guys were pulled apart. In the rush to evacuate the area, I was jostled to the side, falling hard on my hip. A smash of pain surged from the bruised area, and I yelped.

"This is unacceptable! You're all suspended!" the principal bellowed to the guys.

Josh, Ben, and Quentin were separately led back down the bleachers, surrounded by a posse of grown-ups. I could see the guys straining their heads to spot Maya, but from what I could tell, she wasn't in her seat anymore. Was she still here?

A high musical note pierced the air, sustaining for several

seconds. The crowd turned to the sound, then froze in place.

Was that . . . Maya? I spotted her. She'd moved to the middle of the game floor and was facing the crowd, playing her solo.

I was floored. The old Maya from two weeks ago would have melted in a puddle of embarrassment. But this new, more confident Maya had managed to push the fighting and drama aside and was currently playing a kick-ass solo.

As she performed her piece, her fingers flying with deft skill, the crowd remained eerily silent. I'd heard her play before, but never had it been with such strength. Such confidence.

After another minute or so, the last note burst forth, then stopped. Maya pulled the trumpet from her mouth, dragging in a deep breath.

The crowd went wild, screaming with approval and applause.

Maya nodded her head slightly in thanks, then turned and exited the auditorium without a backward glance.

My hip aching in pain, I dropped my head in my hands, fighting back the shaky nerves that threatened to take over. What a nightmare I'd caused.

How was I ever gonna fix this?

Chapter 19

With a heavy sigh, I keyed my front door and dragged myself into the house. After the basketball game disaster, Maya had called Andy to tell us she just wanted to go home and sleep, so we'd decided to cancel our TGIF sleepover.

Honestly, I couldn't blame her, as I was feeling a little shell-shocked myself. So, I'd just headed home . . . alone, with my horny parents. Great, more fun times for me. The only way this evening could get any better would be if a meteor suddenly hit our house.

I took off my shoes in the foyer and made my way into the living room. Mom and Dad were cuddling on the couch. The room was dark except for the flickering screen of whatever black and white movie they were watching.

"Oh, you're home?" Flashes of light from the TV flitted across Mom's surprised face. Her hair was slightly mussed, and I realized I must have interrupted them mid-makeout.

Gross. Every teen's worst nightmare, now my daily existence. Just another one of my brilliant matchmaking ideas. At least the spell wouldn't last forever. Right now, that was my only saving grace.

I fought the urge to shudder. "Yeah, I'm just going to bed." I slung my purse over my shoulder.

"But I thought you were staying at Andy's tonight," Dad said.

"We decided to hold off until next week." I shrugged like there was no problem. I didn't want to share the basketball game drama with them. "Not a big deal."

"Well, that's too bad," she said, glancing at Dad with a tender smile on her face. "Your father and I just got back from that Japanese restaurant. He treated me to a date, and it's not even our anniversary yet—wasn't that nice of him? The food was fantastic."

Dad shrugged, sliding a strand of Mom's hair out of her eyes. "It was okay, I guess. I liked it more than I thought I would."

"So why did you go, then?" I asked him.

"I knew it would make your mom happy," he said. "And why wait until our anniversary to show her how much I care?"

She made love-sick eyes at him. "Oh, Stephen."

"You're worth it."

They kissed. UGH. I took my cue and booked it upstairs. After tossing my purse on my computer chair and draping across my bed, I buried my face in my bedspread and replayed the whole evening in my mind.

Why had things turned out like this with Operation Hook Maya Up? Was there something I could have done to prevent this disaster? I mean, besides not having orchestrated it in the first place. It was obvious by now that I should have just picked one guy from the start and run with it. But they'd all seemed so right for her.

I thought about the events of the last two weeks. All three boys had made Maya feel special and important, but she'd run around like a chicken with its head cut off, looking more and more frazzled every day.

I rolled over onto my back, pondering Dad's words. He didn't want to go to the Japanese restaurant, but he'd gone because my mom had wanted it. My parents' relationship since the cupid spell had blossomed in a direction I wasn't thrilled about, but it was showing me something I hadn't thought about before.

Real love was giving, compromising with someone, like what

my dad did for my mom. Maya and the guys had all bent over backward to do stuff for each other, but it wasn't the *right* stuff, the one thing to truly make her happy. None of the boys seemed to complete Maya with his presence the way Mom and Dad did for each other.

I grabbed my nightclothes together and headed to the bathroom to take a quick shower, a bit more enlightened than before. This selflessness thing was definitely something to watch for with my future matches. Maybe keeping these new ideas about love in mind could help me even learn to predict how well my matches would turn out.

This cupid job wasn't as easy as I'd first thought, but I was totally figuring it out. My future matches were going to be so much better now—I just knew it.

School on Monday came and went, with Maya nowhere in sight. She hadn't returned any of my calls over the weekend, so Andy and I had spent the lunch period fretting over Maya's state of mental health.

Was she buried in her bed under her blanket, crying her eyes out? Was she blaming me and Andy for our dating advice? Worry picked away at my nerves, making me edgy and tense.

To make matters worse, Andy told me she had found out Maya's guys had been suspended for a week. What a mess. At least the spell would end today, so things could level out for everyone involved.

Art class had offered me no happy reprieve, either. Derek wasn't in class today because of some other school project, so I slogged through the period bored and without my daily visual stimulation.

When the bell rang, I exited the building by myself. I noticed Britney leaning against the wall, her back facing me.

"Hey," I said to her as I approached.

She turned and smiled. "Oh, hey, Felicity."

A loud clanging sound rang out from the side of the building. I peeked my head around the corner. Sure enough, there was Matthew and his new girl doing his favorite pastime, garbage diving. They were enthusiastically tossing recyclables out of the bins, their cheeks bright red from the cold sting of the air.

"So . . . how are you?" I asked Britney, studying her face. She didn't seem overly distraught, nor did she look like she'd been crying. In fact, she looked serene.

"You know, I thought I'd be more upset seeing them together. But honestly, I'm just happy I'm not in the trash." Her smile grew bigger. "Let them have their bonding time together. That just doesn't work for me."

"I don't blame you," I said, chuckling. "There are better ways to spend time than smelling like a landfill."

"Well, I'm heading home. See ya." Tossing one last look over her shoulder at Matthew, she shook her head, then walked off.

I walked home too, feeling better for the first time in days. Yeah, Britney's matchmaking didn't end romantically, but it did end happily. She was moving on, finding her inner strength. That was definitely something I would share in my weekly work meeting tonight.

"Seems like things are moving along for you," Janet said to me later that afternoon, propping her elbows on her desk and steepling her fingers. "You made another match last week, right?"

I nodded, trying to keep my nervousness under control. Though Janet didn't know exactly what had happened with Maya's matchmaking, I'd 'fessed up that Britney's coupling didn't work out, and that Maya's pairing also failed.

But to help take the focus off all the bad, I'd made sure to talk about how DeShawn had shown positive progress over the last twelve days while paired with Marisa, how closely knit Mallory and Bobby had become, and how Britney had changed too.

Janet smiled. "Well, I'm proud of the work you've done so far."

My heart thudded in surprise from her praise, and my shoulders sagged in relief. "Really? Thanks. It's been a lot harder than I expected."

"It sure is. You should have seen me the first few months I began to matchmake. I was a total wreck, afraid every couple I'd paired up would fail."

"You?" It was hard to imagine the pristine, perfectly composed Janet as anxious. She was the pinnacle of self-confidence.

"Absolutely." Janet winked. "We all start out unsure of ourselves. But I have something to help take your mind off your matchmaking woes." She flipped open a folder on her desk and handed me a paycheck.

Yay! Getting money perked me up a bit. "Thank you." I stuffed the check in my purse. "So, you're not upset that some of my couples didn't stay together?"

Janet leaned toward me. "You know, I've made many people fall in and out of love during my time, and every pairing I make continues to surprise me. Our ability as cupids to cause that . . .

spark, that instant connection between two people, doesn't guarantee a couple will stay together." She paused. "One thing you should always remember, Felicity, is that love isn't a science. It's not predictable, though we'd like it to be. And love can work out between even the unlikeliest of people, as well as fail spectacularly between couples who seem ideal for each other."

No kidding. And Wednesday would show me if one of those unpredictable couples, DeShawn and Marisa, would make it or not.

Still half asleep on Wednesday morning, I headed into the school building, taking off my jacket and cramming it into my locker. I took out my *Jane Eyre* novel and headed to first-period English, praying Maya would be there. Yesterday had also come and gone still without a word from her, and I was starting to get sick from worry.

Maya still wasn't here. I slipped into my seat and anxiously watched the door, drumming my fingers on the top of the desk. I didn't know what I was going to say to her, but I needed to do something.

The bell rang, and Maya came through the door just in time,

much to my relief. She parked it in the seat beside me. I tried to catch her attention, but she was busy getting her notebook and class supplies out. When I leaned over to whisper to her, Mrs. Kendel saw me and gave me the evil eye, so I straightened back up and faced forward.

Why wasn't Maya looking at me? Maybe she'd realized I was involved in her love-life disasters and was furious with me.

Oh God, what if she'd found out I was a cupid? This week was getting worse and worse.

Mrs. Kendel started class talking about *Jane Eyre*, but I didn't care. Once my paranoid thoughts had taken over, they wouldn't let me go.

Maya scribbled quickly on a piece of paper, then ripped it out, folded it up, and deftly slipped it to me.

Heart in throat, I read its contents:

So sry didn't call. Bad few days, but better now. Tlk after class?

I nearly cried in sweet relief. Maya didn't hate me, and it didn't appear that she'd figured out about the cupid stuff. I wrote *Yup!* on the bottom of the page and handed it back to her, then opened my novel, ready to focus on the lecture.

In between taking notes, I kept a close eye on DeShawn too. The spell had worn off today, but his quiet demeanor gave me no indication of what was happening between him and Marisa. Talk about a killer poker face.

Were they still together? Had her friends convinced her to dump him? Maybe after class, I could keep my eyes peeled for Marisa in the hallway.

When the bell rang forty minutes later, I gathered my stuff and moved out the classroom door, tugging Maya along with me.

"You okay?" I asked her, scanning the hallway quickly for Marisa to see if she'd meet DeShawn. I didn't see her, so I focused my attention back on Maya.

She nodded slowly. "I am now. I just needed some down time."

"I'm sorry." And I was. It had to have been a rough weekend for her. Poor Maya.

"Hey," Andy said, popping up between us. She hugged Maya, then pulled back, a frown on her face. "I've been worried about you."

"Sorry for the disappearing act." Maya smiled. "I fretted over the guys all weekend about what to do. If I should call them to apologize and explain so I could patch everything up. But when I woke up on Monday, it was like I didn't feel that . . . pressure anymore. That overwhelming desire to be with them."

"That's crazy." Andy shook her head. "But probably better for your sanity."

"I know it," Maya said. "All this time, I've been worrying over which was the perfect guy for me, and then I realized: None of them is. It was fun to date them, but maybe the reason I couldn't choose which one to keep is that none of them was all the things I want in a boyfriend. But I wasn't ready to face everyone at school yet because of Friday night's incident, so I told my mom I was sick. Luckily, she let me stay home."

"I think I understand what you mean," I said, wondering if the guys had also fallen out of love when the spell wore off, or if they'd continue to fight over her and try to win her back.

"So what now?" Andy asked. "Are you planning to date any of them again?"

"No, I think I'm done with them," Maya answered. "I liked their attention, but none of them were quite right for me, though it seemed like it at first." She paused, then said, "Hey, can you guys hang on a sec?"

Maya darted across the hallway to talk to a familiar-looking guy who was standing by the lockers. It was the mysterious new guy from her French class, the one whose name I needed for my profile.

"Um, do you have yesterday's assignment?" Maya asked him.

"Whoa," Andy whispered to me. "Is that *our* friend Maya, going up to talk to a guy?"

"It would appear so." The Maya from two weeks ago never would have done that. I loved seeing this new boldness, this confidence in her.

"Damn, I gotta run to class. Fill me in later on everything that happens," Andy ordered, hugging me quickly. She disappeared into the hallway.

"Oh, hey," the guy said to Maya, surprise flushing his cheeks a deep red. "Yeah, I do." He dropped his backpack onto the ground and hunched over to dig into it. Books and papers filled with writing were crammed in there. How in the world did he find anything?

"Here you go," he finally said as he stood, thrusting a piece of paper at her. Did I detect a slight shake in his hand?

"Thanks," Maya replied, giving him a small smile. She drew in a deep breath and swallowed. Her eyes darted to the ground, then back to him again.

Wait, was Maya flirting? I leaned back against the locker, watching the melodrama of teenage life unfold right before my eyes.

"So, maybe we can get together sometime and study for the French test," Maya continued. "If-if you want, I mean." Her cheeks turned a light shade of pink.

The guy nodded, giving her a toothy grin. "Yeah, I'd like that. Maybe we can meet today?"

"Let's meet tonight at Pizza Hut at . . . seven? We can eat and study."

"Okay." He grinned even wider, if that was possible.

Maya headed back toward me, then threw out over her shoulder to the guy, "See ya then."

I nestled my books in front of my chest and regarded her with one eyebrow raised. Well, well, well. This was an interesting turn of events.

"What was *that* all about?" I probed, understanding full well what was going on. Mama didn't raise no fool.

She shrugged a bit too casually. "Oh, nothing much. He's Scott Baker, from my French class. We're going to study together tonight."

"I see." And suddenly, I realized that Maya probably had been interested in this Scott guy before I hit her with the Operation Hook Maya Up love spell. After all, this sudden awareness of him hadn't come out of nowhere.

Whoops.

Well, she hadn't told me, so there was no way I could have known before pairing her up with the other guys.

But all's well that ends well, right? At least things were going in the right direction for her now. And the spell did play a part in that.

I knew, though, that things didn't end that well for Quentin, Josh, and Ben, even if it wasn't my fault how crazy they got under the spell . . . well, not 100 percent my fault, anyway. Besides, I totally learned my lesson. Once the guys were off suspension, maybe I could start to make amends by finding them appropriate girlfriends—one for each of them, of course.

Maya and I moved back down the hallway, splitting up to head to our respective classes. Across the hallway from my American history classroom, I spotted Marisa standing with her friends.

Instantly, I stopped mid-stride, then darted in front of some nearby lockers to scope the situation.

"—too bad," Marisa was saying to them. "DeShawn's changed. I've seen the difference in him, even if you refuse to believe it."

So Marisa was still in love, even after the spell wore off? Sweet bliss! That was one half of the battle.

One of her friends shook her head, her arms crossed in front of her. "He's just putting on an act."

"No, he isn't," Marisa replied, her lips pursed and her brow furrowed. "Look, I know you guys care about me, but I need friends who support me, even if they don't agree with what I choose to do." She hitched her books on her hip. "I hope you'll think about that."

Marisa stepped into the hallway toward DeShawn, who reached out and took her hand.

I watched the two of them walk off into the sunset. Okay, they were just heading to their classes—but still, it felt romantic and utterly fulfilling to see their fingers tightly woven together as they strolled down the hall.

I was amazed. Marisa had stood up to her friends and chose what she felt was best for herself. She hadn't caved to their pressure.

And just as cool for me, I'd made a match last past the two-week spell! There was hope after all, both for love and for my matchmaking career. And, oh yeah, for my wallet.

I slipped into American history. Once I got into my seat, I dug my trusty PDA out and created a quick profile for the new guy Scott Baker, then sent a love e-mail to both him and Maya. Just to nudge things along a bit.

I pushed the LoveLine 3000 back into my bag and leaned back with a satisfied smile while Mr. Shrupe started class. Things were going to be better now, I just knew it. Quentin, Josh, and Ben would be out of suspension tomorrow—and now that the love spell had worn off, their lives could go back to normal too. That had to be a big relief to them.

I just hoped they'd be able to let it go and not stay mad at each other. And if not, I'd find a way to make that happen.

Of course, I couldn't just sit back and rest on my laurels. More love matches had to be made. After all, the DeShawn-Marisa match had worked, so I knew I had the ability to make good couples. And if that weren't enough proof, my parents' renewed interest in each other, to put it politely, was icing on the cake.

And if their relationship ever flagged again, I could do another love match for my folks to spice things up a bit . . . and then send myself on a two-week trip so I wouldn't have to watch.

I flipped my social studies book open and wrote in my notebook as Mr. Shrupe scrawled across the chalk board, wiping a chalk-dusted hand on the left buttcheek of his brown pants. I bit back a giggle. Good old Mr. Shrupe—at least he never changed.

While Mr. Shrupe droned on, I peered out the window and saw Derek walk by outside with a group of jocks, his letterman jacket hugging his upper body nicely. He laughed at something one of the guys said, a dimple creasing his cheek. My heart slammed in my chest at the unexpected pleasure of seeing him.

Derek sauntered off with his friends, and I drew a heart-shaped doodle in the margin of my notes. Watching Maya grab the bull by the horns and ask Scott out had inspired me. If I was going to snag Derek for myself, I needed to bring my A-game. I knew he would be the perfect guy for me.

It was going to be a challenge, since I couldn't use my cupid skills, but aren't the best things in life the ones you worked for?

Absolutely. And I was totally ready.

Who will be Felicity's next love ~~disaster~~ match?

Flirting with Disaster

"There are lots of fun ways to have a good time at a party without drinking!" Mrs. Cahill, our health class teacher, hopped up on the end of her large desk. She crossed her legs beneath a flowing brown paisley skirt.

A few people chuckled at her words, and I bit back a laugh myself. At least she was enthusiastic about her topic. It was hard for me to scrape up enthusiasm for anything on a Monday, but Mrs. Cahill never lacked any.

"So, what did you guys list?" Mrs. Cahill asked. "Let's share a few of our choices with the class. Now as I said before, I won't be collecting them. This is for you to take home and hopefully implement in your life to encourage a lifestyle that avoids alcohol."

Yeah, right. I was sure most of my classmates would instantly give up partying because of a list made in health class. That was *totally* plausible.

I glanced down at my paper. Our in-class assignment was to write ten "fun" things to do that didn't involve alcohol. Out of my ten items, six of them involved staring longingly at Derek, the guy I've been madly in love with since freshman year. No way was I going to say that out loud, though.

James Powers thrust his hand into the air, a smarmy grin on his face.

"Go ahead, James," Mrs. Cahill said. "What did you write?"

He made a big show of holding up his paper in front of his face. "Ahem. I put, 'Have sex.'"

His buddies around him guffawed, and several girls tittered behind their hands. I rolled my eyes. Mrs. Cahill should have known better than to call on James.

"Oh my God, James!" one girl whispered, giggling. "You're so crazy."

Mrs. Cahill blushed and pressed a hand to her beet-red cheeks. "Well, that's . . . not quite what I meant."

Mallory Robinson, my mortal enemy and the bane of my

existence, turned and whispered something to her friends, Jordan and Carrie. Jordan nodded briefly in response, but Carrie barely looked at her. They both turned their attention back to James. Mallory's face fell. She quickly recovered and started writing in her notebook.

I smirked. The dynamics between Mallory and her friends had changed ever since I'd set her up last month with Bobby Loward, aka Bobby Blowhard, the biggest weenie I'd ever known. It was still the most talked-about love match around school, even though the magic had worn off and Mallory and Bobby had split up a few weeks ago.

Of course, nobody else knew that there'd been magic involved in their hookup, let alone that I was the cupid responsible for the match. Total secrecy was the first rule of my job at Cupid's Hollow. I wasn't allowed to tell a soul that my hot-pink PDA was used to matchmake my classmates using the latest in handheld technology—love arrows shot through e-mail.

Not that anyone would believe me if I *were* allowed to spill the beans. Though maybe the ridiculous pairing of Mallory and Bobby Blowhard would be convincing proof.

Mallory's friends hadn't treated her the same since. It didn't matter that they'd broken up the day the spell wore off. The damage was already done.

My only regret was that I couldn't step forward and claim credit for what was surely an act of humanity: keeping Mallory's stuck-up nose out of my best friend Maya Takahashi's dating life by giving Mallory a relationship of her own to focus on. But the cupid contract I'd signed meant I couldn't spill the beans—and frankly, I feared my boss Janet too much to screw around with that.

"What about spin the bottle, then?" Mitzi, one of the flaky chicks in our class, asked. "That's just making out, not actually *doing* it."

Andy Carsen, my other best friend, bit back a laugh. She leaned over and whispered to me, "I think the whole point of the exercise was to *avoid* bottles."

"No kidding," I said quietly, shaking my head.

Mrs. Cahill looked over at me. "Felicity, since you feel like talking, do you have anything to add to our conversation? What did you write down on your list?"

Whoops. I glanced at my paper, reading aloud an entry that wouldn't totally humiliate me for life. "Um, play poker."

Not that I knew how to play, but I don't think that mattered to her. At least I didn't say something that involved being naked.

"Good answer!" Mrs. Cahill beamed at me. "Card games are a fun and healthy alternative to drinking at a party."

"What an ass kisser," I heard Mallory whisper to her friends. They giggled.

Andy spun around in her seat and stared hard at Mallory until she looked away.

The bell rang, dismissing us from class.

"Make sure you hold on to those lists," Mrs. Cahill said loudly over the bell as we all rushed to evacuate. "Especially since we're nearing prom season."

"Thank *God* that's over," I said to Andy as we walked down the hall. "I swear, that class gets weirder every day."

"No kidding," Andy said. "I don't think Mrs. Cahill was expecting those responses. She should know James by now, though. He's always going to give the most obnoxious answers he can think of."

"You know, I'd feel bad for her if she hadn't given us this dumb assignment in the first place."

I hated health class with the fiery passion of a thousand burning suns. It was possibly the most boring, ineffective course I'd taken to date. The only good thing about it was I didn't have to take gym anymore, one of the other most terrible classes ever.

I was so not athletic, and it was highly unfair that I was forced to participate in events that made me look like a dumbass. Ever see me dribble a basketball? Once you did, you'd understand my plight.

But health class was not much better. For one period every day I was trapped in a room with both James and Bobby. And even worse, with Mallory, who took every opportunity to shoot me nasty glares across the room, or make snotty comments to her friends.

In between shooting me the evil eye, Mallory would sneak peeks at James, who was her boyfriend freshman year. She was probably wondering why they weren't still together. Um, maybe because she was a total cow. Not that James even noticed her anymore. He was too busy trying to show the whole class how very funny he was.

Fortunately, Andy was in there with me. She helped make the time go faster with her dry humor.

"Hey, Felicity, that was a good answer," Bobby Blowhard, said, appearing out of nowhere and sliding in between me and Andy. "I didn't know you played poker. What's your favorite kind? I like Texas Hold'em."

Fortunately for us, and all of mankind, Bobby wasn't wearing his usual mesh workout shirt. Instead he had on a tight black spandex top. I suppose it was his way of enticing people to look at his muscles, but I can't say it worked on me.

"Actually, I don't really play," I mumbled, trying not to be rude, but also not wanting to encourage him into further conversation.

Bobby was . . . overbearing, to say the least. I'd noticed that once the cupid spell wore off him, he lost his attraction toward Mallory and instantly regained it toward me.

Lucky, lucky me.

"Oh." Bobby paused and flexed a little. "Well, maybe I could teach you sometime. I know lots of card games, actually, and—"

"Hey," Andy interrupted, "it's time for us to head to lunch." She grabbed my elbow and led me away.

"Okay, see ya!" Bobby bellowed to my back.

I gave him a halfhearted wave as Andy and I darted down the hall.

"I owe you," I told her gratefully. "Cokes are on me."

We headed to the cafeteria and made our way through the lunch line to our usual table, where Maya was already waiting for us. She was holding hands and talking closely with her boyfriend of almost a month, Scott Baker.

I swear, the guy looked like he had a permanent flush whenever he was around Maya. It was cute, even if it was a little goofy. But it made me happy to see her with a guy who was perfect for her.

After the fiasco of matching her up with three guys at once, I'd learned the hard way that it was much better to do a one-on-one pairing. Much, *much* better. Maya had started dating Scott after that, and they'd been going strong since. Of course I had sent them a cupid e-mail to encourage their attraction (not that they'd needed it).

And just as cool, I'd recently received my second bonus check for a lasting love match. Score!

"Hey," Andy said, plopping down beside Maya. "How's my favorite couple today?"

"Oh, hey guys!" Maya shot us a big smile. "How are you? Anything good going on?"

"Not too much," I said. "Except in health class James said he wanted to have sex instead of drink at a party, and Mrs. Cahill about had a heart attack." I sat on Andy's other side and started noshing on my burrito.

Maya shook her head. "Yeah, that sounds like him. And more exciting than my morning."

"Actually Maya got an A on her French test," Scott interjected. "She beat all of us with the top score. She could probably teach our class and put Monsieur LeBec out of a job."

Maya shrugged, blushing. "I guess you're just a good study partner," she replied. She glanced at her watch, then stood. "Oh, I gotta go. I told Mr. Seagle I'd help him set up the chem lab today before class."

"I'll go with you," Scott said, automatically rising beside her.

"You two lovebirds have fun. Try not to coo all over each other," Andy ribbed.

Maya shot her a fake glare. "Funny, funny."

She and Scott headed out of the cafeteria, glued to each others' sides. I couldn't help but grin at the sight of them.

"If I didn't love Maya so much, I'd be super jealous," Andy said, watching them go.

"She looks so happy."

I jerked my head to look at her. "Jealous? Really? I thought you'd sworn off love."

Andy bit her lower lip. She drew lines in her creamed corn with her fork. Why the school was serving creamed corn with burritos, I'd never know.

"I thought so too," she said with a sigh, "but seeing how good they are together makes me think, maybe I'm missing out on something."

My heart rate kick-started to about a million beats a minute. Andy had been on a self-imposed sabbatical from guys for a while now and hadn't shown any interest in dating. So this was the opportunity I'd been waiting for—to hear her say she was ready for me to find her a love match.

Okay, not that she knew I'd be matchmaking her, but whatever. I knew I could do the job justice. After all, Maya and Scott were still going strong, as were DeShawn and Marisa, an unlikely couple I'd paired on a whim who seemed to beat all odds and make it work. That relationship had also changed DeShawn's bad attitude, and he wasn't the uber-butthead he used to be.

I just knew I could help Andy find love too.

"Yeah, Scott seems like living proof that there are nice guys out there," I said casually.

"No kidding. If only we could all be so lucky. She snagged herself a good one." Andy took a bite of her food, then shot me a pointed look. "Not that *you* won't be that lucky soon, with you-know-who."

My stomach flipped over in excitement at the thought of Derek smiling at me the way Scott smiled at Maya. God, would there ever be a time when Derek didn't make every part of me feel utterly, painfully alive? A time when I wasn't a total wreck, wishing I could get him to see me as the perfect match for him?

For the thousandth time since taking the cupid job, I rued the fact that I couldn't matchmake myself.

"Well, who knows what'll happen with that," I said, biting off a big hunk of my burrito. I chewed and swallowed before speaking again. "Our plan of me repeatedly throwing myself in front of him hasn't seemed to work yet."

Not only had Derek *not* fallen head over heels in love and dropped down on one knee to ask me out on a date, things hadn't progressed much further than the casual conversation stage we had been at for a couple of months now. It was slow torture, and yet I was putting myself willingly through it every step of the way.

"Well, maybe we'll both be surprised." Andy shot me a crooked smile. "Maybe love will strike us both out of the blue."

I grinned back. "If it can happen for Maya, it surely will happen for you."

Because I'd sure see to it that it would.

About the Author

Rhonda Stapleton started writing a few years ago to appease the voices in her head. She lives in northwest Ohio with her two kids, her manpanion, and their lazy dog. Visit her website at RhondaStapleton.com, or drop her a line at rhonda@rhondastapleton.com.